Erotica 3:
Bettina's Playtime

Erotica 3:
Bettina's Playtime

collected by
Bettina Varese

**COLLECTIVE
PUBLISHING**

Copyright © COLLECTIVE PUBLISHING

First published in 2001 by
COLLECTIVE PUBLISHING

ISBN 0 9535290 2 9

Stories collected by Bettina Varese
Edited by Judy Keaton & Simon Starkwell
Designed and Typeset by Collective Publishing

Printed and bound in Great Britain
by Cox and Wyman Ltd
Reading, Berkshire

COLLECTIVE PUBLISHING
P.O. Box 6685, Newark, NG24 4WS, United Kingdom
www.collectivepublishing.com

COLLECTIVE
PUBLISHING

ENGLAND

Bettina writes,

I always carry a condom wherever I go.
Make sure you also practise safe sex.

Contents

Contents

Contents

Dear Reader,

Welcome to my third book of erotic stories. I hope that like me, you have had many wonderful, sexy experiences in the year since my last book came out. I am so excited to bring you another hot selection of sexy tales.

I hope you like this, my latest collection.

Love as always

Bettina writes,

Welcome to the first story.

Now, you know I like to try different things - all in the name of research you understand - well, to me there's nothing better than getting in front of the camera and posing for some sexy pictures, you can just forget yourself and become a fantasy.

Well, I decided it was about time I experienced it from the other side of the lens. I know how to handle a camera, so I booked a studio and picked out some sexy girls from a model agency. One of the models was Katrina. She really is stunning and the sexiest model I photographed. A real girl-next-door type, and she always has that little bit more to give you.

While we were shooting she told me how she got into modelling . . .

I couldn't help it,
I needed the money

I COULDN'T HELP IT, I NEEDED THE MONEY

I couldn't help it, I needed the money. My family all live in the Midlands and I'm having to survive on my own, living in a squalid bedsit in Twickenham, and what a dump that is. I'm four weeks behind in the rent and the landlord keeps hassling me for the money, says if I can't find it, I can pay him in kind. The dirty bastard.

I saw the advert in one of those teen girl magazines, it was hidden away amongst the personal ads. The advert read,

> 'Young girls wanted by film maker -
> Must be good looking and broad-minded-
> Good money to be made'.

Well my friends say I'm attractive and I think I'm broad-minded, and I definitely needed the money, so I rang the number and decided to go along. The guy gave me his address and said to come by to see if I was suitable. He didn't really tell me much about it on the phone, just said to come along on Monday morning and to bring a friend if I wanted.

My best friend at college, Ann, couldn't come with me as she had a tutorial that morning, so I decided to go on my own. I mean what could happen? She knew where

I was going, and he's hardly likely to try anything funny I told her.

I caught the bus towards South London, and got off in Peckham. I had the A to Z and soon found the house. It was old and a little run down, the front garden was a bit overgrown. I walked up the pathway, took a deep breath and knocked on the door. To my surprise it was opened by a girl about my age. She was very pretty, long blonde hair. She was dressed in a nurses uniform - not a real one but a sex shop kind of one, a bit tacky. Around her neck she had a stethoscope.

"Come in, come in, are you here to see Adrian?"

"Yes," I said, "he's the guy who makes the films right?"

"Yes, come through, follow me, we were just about to start filming - I'm playing a naughty nurse, I expect you guessed!"

We walked up two flights of stairs and were met by a tall guy with a slightly receding hairline.

"Are you Katrina?" he asked.

"Yes, I've come along to have a look really, and for you to meet me - we spoke on the phone."

"Well, from the advert you can tell that what you'd be making is a sex film, so you probably know that already?"

"Yes, I suppose I kind of worked that out."

"Yes, well, I make masturbation movies. I put them on to video, they sell really well on the internet, so you are paid very well, two hundred pounds for an afternoons work - what do you think of that?"

"Sounds very generous, but I don't think I could - you know - do it! Of course I do it, but you know not in front of people." I started to blush.

"Don't be too hasty, stay and watch Nikki - you don't mind if Katrina stays do you Nikki?"

"Oh, no I don't mind at all, I love to have an audience," Nikki replied smiling at me.

"Take a seat over there Katrina, and we'll start," Adrian said looking through the camera which was on a tripod. There were two lights aimed at the ceiling.

Nikki looked in the mirror to check her makeup and carefully put on a last coat of lipstick. She had put her long blonde hair up, and the nurses cap sat neatly on top. She sat on the end of a bed and Adrian began to film her. She started talking. She was talking just to the camera and pretending that it was the 'patient'.

"Now, Mr Jones," she began in a chastising voice, "you know I'm not allowed to give you hand relief so there's no use keep asking me. I know you haven't had sex for six weeks and that erection does look pretty painful, but rules are rules." Nikki picked up a clipboard and pen from the bed as if she was about to write on it. Then she thought for a moment, putting the pen to her lips. "I know, I've got an idea, I'll unbandage your right hand - I'm sure the matron won't mind, just for half an hour, it might do that nasty rash of yours a bit of good. I'll put on a little show for you and well, you can relieve yourself. We can both have a bit of fun at the same time."

Nikki stood up.

3

"Do you like what I'm wearing Mr Jones? I bet you do - you know what I think Mr Jones, I think you fantasize about me all day - I think you want to get inside my knickers, don't you Mr Jones. Well, there's only one hand going in my panties, Mr Jones, and that's mine."

Nikki lifted the hem of her tiny dress and showed Mr Jones her panties. They were pink cotton with a white trim.

"Do you like them Mr Jones? Yes they're pretty aren't they - I've been on duty for eight hours and they're very hot Mr Jones."

Nikki ran a finger between her legs.

"Very, *very* hot!"

"If you're a good boy and come when I do, I might let you have these. What about my tits Mr Jones, would you like to see them?"

Nikki then sat in a leatherette armchair next to the bed, you know the kind, leatherette back and seat with metal arms. She slowly pulled the zipper down on her outfit revealing a matching pink brassiere.

"I bet you'd love to get your dick between these Mr Jones, I know I'd love to feel it hard between my tits, pushing up and down until you ejaculated, coming all over my tits."

To my surprise I was getting really turned on, I squeezed my thighs together, crossing and uncrossing my legs to get as much pressure on my pussy as I could without making it too obvious.

Nikki unclipped her bra and tossed it towards the camera. Her nipples were hard and erect, and she was massaging them, flicking the tips with her long manicured fingernails. Dipping her head forward she took one breast in her mouth and sucked and licked, pulling at the nipple with her teeth.

"Ooh Mr Jones, that feels so sexy, my pussy is getting really wet. I can see your dick is lovely and hard, that's right keep running your hand up and down the shaft Mr Jones. But remember, don't come just yet. I'll tell you when."

Nikki went back to massaging her tits, my own pussy was wet with her words. She took a bottle of what looked like sun cream from the top of the bedside cabinet and squeezed some out onto her breasts.

"Oh Mr Jones, that feels so good . . . I'm imagining that you've come . . . all over my tits Mr Jones, I'm rubbing your cream into my tits . . . oh it feels so *good*."

Nikki carried on doing this for a couple of minutes till the white sticky liquid had all vanished.

"Now Mr Jones," said Nikki as she pulled the zipper on the front of her uniform right down, "I'm going to play with my pussy until I come - it's already so wet!"

Nikki eased her bottom up off the seat and pulled her panties down to just below her knees.

"There Mr Jones, can you see, my pussy is *so* wet!"

Nikki slid a finger between her sex lips and then licked it.

"Mmm, that tastes so sweet."

I had never seen anything so sexy, so erotic. I found

5

myself imagining what it would be like to be kneeling between her open legs eating her pussy, tasting her sweet girly-cum on my tongue. My own pussy was burning hot, my panties were soaked, hopelessly trying to put out the fire.

"Mmm, Mr Jones, my clit is so hard and tender."

Nikki had two fingers in her cunt and her other hand was playing with her clitoris, rubbing and pulling, making her squirm. She lifted her bottom off the chair pushing her pussy up onto her fingers.

"Ooh, yes, yes, Mr Jones - I'm coming - that's it faster Mr Jones - I want to see you come. Oh I'm coming . . . now . . . now . . . ooh yes, yes, yes, ooh yes . . ."

I could see Nikki's cum trickling from her pussy, a creamy white. She sat back in the chair, her legs and pussy spread wide. Her eyes closed.

"Well Mr Jones, did you enjoy that? Oh dear, I can see you made a bit of a mess there," she said smiling, "it seems to be everywhere, here let me clean you up."

Nikki got up from the chair and walked towards the camera and out of shot.

"Brilliant Nikki!" announced Adrian.

Nikki picked up her clothes and started to dress.

"Give me a ring when you're next free then Nikki. Here's your money for today, I've put it on the table for you."

"Thanks Adrian. I'll probably give you a call in a couple of weeks. I've always liked the look of that police womans outfit you've got hanging over there. Perhaps I could do something in that, using the truncheon?" Nikki stepped out from behind the screen still doing up the zip on her skirt.

"Yeah, that would be good - don't forget your money. See you in a couple of weeks then, sweetheart."

Nikki picked up the money. Without counting it she stuffed it in her handbag. Turning to me she said, "Maybe we could do a double act if you fancy it - that would sell well wouldn't it Adrian? The punters love the girl/girl stuff don't they?"

"They sure do. Are you interested Katrina?"

"I'm not sure, I'd have to think about it. I've never done anything with a girl before. I'm not sure that I'd know what to do."

"We'd only kiss, play with each other a bit, and maybe use some toys, it'd be fun," Nikki said smiling.

"Don't pressure Katrina, let her think about it for a couple of days."

"Okay, I'll see you soon, ta-ra."

Nikki picked up her bags and left.

"Well Katrina, do you think you could do as well as Nikki? It's not easy doing it in front of the camera, and it has to be real, it's obvious if you fake it. The camera never lies."

I thought for a moment, I really needed the money, and I'd rather do it with myself or Nikki, than with my fat, greasy landlord. At least this way I'd keep my self-respect.

"Yes, I'll do it. I'll do it now!"

"Okay, great. We'll just do a straight bed scene as it's your first go. Pick something off the rail over there and then we'll start."

I walked over to the rail and picked out a matching red bra and panty set. I went behind the screen, took off my clothes and put on the underwear. My own panties were soaked. I looked in my handbag for a tissue to wipe my pussy before putting on the new pair. Everything fitted really well, and my boobs were lifted up into a really tight cleavage. I took a deep breath and stepped out from behind the screen.

"You look fantastic! Now, what I want you to do is to just be aware of yourself and the camera. Don't look anywhere else in the room, pretend your lover is the camera, and you're putting on a show for him. Talk, if you feel you're confident enough. We'll just see how it goes, treat it as a bit of fun. All right sweetheart?" Adrian's manner was very reassuring.

"Okay Adrian, let's give it a shot."

Adrian got back behind the camera. I couldn't believe what I was about to do - masturbate in front of a complete stranger - although because he was a stranger, it somehow made it easier. I'd never touched myself in front of anyone, not even the couple of boyfriends I'd had, we'd only ever had ordinary sex, never experimented.

I felt I was under no pressure with Adrian, everything was easy going. I sat on the edge of the bed and just started making it up as I went along. The words just seemed to come into my head.

"I'm going to do a little show for you, now you mustn't come over here but you can play with yourself, because that's what I'm going to do. I'm going to masturbate in front of you, I know you like to watch, you do don't you. I've seen you watching me when you thought I wasn't looking."

I smiled at the camera (my lover!) and unclipped my bra, letting it fall onto the bed. I pinched my nipples, and remembering what Nikki had done, I lifted my boob up and licked and sucked till the red nipple was hard and erect. I was beginning to feel at ease, and I started to enjoy myself.

"You want to see my pussy, don't you? Well you have to be patient - I don't want you to think I'm easy - I'm a good girl."

I teased my middle finger down the outside of my panties, pushing and outlining my pussy lips, pausing to caress my clitoris. I closed my eyes and sighed. My confidence increased.

"Oh, that feels good . . . my clit's so responsive, all I have to do is lightly brush it with my finger and it excites me, it sends a tingling feeling through my whole body. That's it, let me see your cock, it's so big and hard. Imagine it's sliding into my pussy. Umm, that feels good doesn't it? Lovely and hot. Push it right in . . . oh yes . . . I want it to fill me . . . oh yes. "

I opened my legs wide and ran both hands underneath each side of the gusset, then let go to hear the knicker elastic snap back into place. I rubbed my clit through the red nylon. I stared straight into the camera, slowly, licking my lipstick covered lips. I was so turned on, one finger inside me, and I would have come straight away.

I'd lost track of the time. I'd never thought of myself as an exhibitionist, but I was really getting off on this. I lay back and lifted my legs so they pointed straight up in the air, then I slowly eased my panties down and bending my knees I slipped them off, kicking them towards the camera. I opened my legs. The feeling I had was fantastic. I felt so alive.

I found the vibrator that Adrian said was under the pillows if I wanted to use it. I ran it up and down the inside of my thighs, being careful not to touch my pussy or I would explode and climax too early. I let the feelings subside a little bit then carried on.

"This is just like your gorgeous cock. I'm going to suck you."

I placed the vibrator down on the bed in front of me, then kneeling forward with my arse in the air, I went down on it.

I'd only ever given a blowjob to one boy before but I think I had a pretty good technique. He seemed to think so, as soon as he was in my mouth he came. It was quite a shock, I wasn't expecting him to come so quick. I swallowed it all. It tasted kind of weird.

"Mmm, you taste lovely," I said looking up, wide-eyed straight at the camera. "You nearly came didn't you. You naughty boy."

I turned around and squatted so my pussy was just

above the tip of the vibrator.

"I'm going to be fucked." I lowered myself and felt the vibrator sliding into me. "Ooh! yes . . . ahh . . ." It felt huge, it was bigger than I thought. I sat right down on it so there was only a tiny bit sticking out. Then lifting myself up I held the vibrator between my fingers and started to ride it. "Ah . . . ooh, yes, your cock is so big . . . yes fuck me, take me, fuck me . . ."

I had to slow down. I lay back on the bed and sucked on the vibrator.

"Do you like my wet pussy? I bet you'd like to taste it?" I teased, licking the vibrator.

"Mmm, you'd love it." I purred, pushing the vibrator into my mouth once more and sucking it like a cock. "I don't know about you but I need to release all this pent up tension. I bet your cock is ready to come. Let's do it together. That's it, faster . . . faster. I want to see you shoot your hot sticky cum all over me. I love to rub it into my tits, taste it in my mouth. "

I opened my mouth and at the same time pushed two fingers deep into my pussy, finger fucking myself, whilst my other hand rubbed my clit.

"Ooh I can't take this much longer, ooh . . . yes, fuck my pussy . . . yes, yes."

It could have only been about sixty seconds before I climaxed. I tried to keep my eye contact with the camera for the whole time. My orgasm subsided and I felt myself relaxing, a feeling of warmth ran through my body. It was only then that I started to feel embarrassed. I began to giggle, and I couldn't look at Adrian right away.

"That was absolutely brilliant Katrina! You were wonderful. And what a great ending. Would you like a coffee? Get dressed and I'll put the kettle on. How do you take it?"

"Oh, white with two sugars, thanks."

"I've got some biscuits somewhere. Oh, here they are. Take one, you'll like these. Well, did you enjoy yourself?

"Yeah, it was fun! I still can't believe I did it."

"You're a natural. Will you come back to do some more? You are so good at it."

"Yeah, I'd love to do some more."

"And how about that girl/girl with Nikki?"

"Why not."

Bettina writes,

> *If you haven't come yet (I know I have!) then*
> *turn to page 120 for*
> *'I couldn't help it - Episode 2: Katrina and Nikki'.*

Bettina writes,

When I was younger I got into some scrapes, but the two girls in this story really know how to behave badly. Reading about their sexy girly games really turned me on.

I'd be a whore for Clare anytime . . .

In Love With Being A Slut !

IN LOVE WITH BEING A SLUT

When I first met Clare, she was already on a dare kick. That's what brought us together. We were on a minibus full of girls, on our way back from a night's clubbing and the bus had pulled up at some lights. There was a gang of lads on the pavement, looking for a taxi, I suppose. They noticed us and the wolf-whistles started. Some of the girls were giving it loads back, showing their tits, and one of the lads came up to the back doors of the bus and pulled them open. The girls were screaming, and somehow the lad got pulled on board. The moment the lights changed, the driver drove off because, I guess, he didn't want a gang of lads in his minibus as well. He'd had enough problems with the girls as it was. As the bus screeched away, the boy tumbled onto the floor next to Clare.

Clare hadn't been involved, just sitting there with her 'butter wouldn't melt in my mouth' look. She had a pale girlish face, and a slim figure, never dressed flashily, never showed much flesh (unlike me, but I'm just a tart really). If you didn't know her, demure was a word you might have used to describe her. Quiet might be another. Once, I even heard a guy call her naive. Clare loved that, she laughed for hours about that one. Demure she was not. Nor quiet. And naive? No! No one seemed to know what to do next. Clare reached down, unzipped the lad's flies, pulled his dick out and said, "Come and get it girls."

The cock was growing visibly in her grasp. Nobody said a word, then one girl giggled and said, "Sit on it then, Clare, come on I dare you!"

Clare's large hazel eyes were glittering, which, later on, I learned always meant something dangerous. She hoisted her short skirt up over her naked arse (I was surprised to see she wasn't wearing even a thong) and lowered herself over the erect cock. The lad was yelling by now, God knows why, because Clare is a looker.

"Someone sit on his face will they?" Clare remarked offhandedly. Well, all the other girls froze. Then, mimicking the giggly girl's voice, she added, "Oh, come on. I *dare* you."

I just decided to go with the flow and lifted my plump but usually well-admired behind right over his head and squished my rather damp knickers right into his face.

There was a big cheer from the other girls.

"Go on Rosie!"

"Ride him Rosie!"

Me and Clare looked at each other from either end of this prone but squirming body and started laughing. Well, the driver (spoilsport) threw the lad out but something had clicked.

After that, Clare and me were inseparable, a girl-gang of two. It seemed at the time we were right for each other. I wanted a mate with a bit of spark, someone who'd egg me on to jump in the deep end and then, when I did, be there right beside me. Someone who knew how to play the game. The game only had one rule, and that rule was: 'Never ever walk away from a dare'. We had to accept any challenge. Okay, a bit of wheedling on the more risky bets was allowed, but I never went completely over the top because I never knew what Clare might come back with later. You might say that me and Clare were a bad influence on each other. We were 'The Girls Who . . .' finish the sentence how you like. The way we saw it, we had reputations to uphold, and the dare stuff was the heart of it all. Didn't matter where, or who you were with, if someone dared you, you did it.

One time we were in the launderette together and I admitted that I thought the man sitting alone down the far end was quite fanciable. Clare smirked and dared me to sneak up and sit next to him, then tell him that I fancied him. My turn to smirk then. What a pathetic dare. Then she told me the rest. I had to make him hard. Tell him I'd love to fuck him and exactly how. Well, of course I did. I got up and walked over as sexily as I could. I leaned forward, pushing my cleavage into his face, and whispered to him. I said that I felt really horny because I hadn't had any cock for ages because my *girlfriend* was very jealous. I said that if she hadn't been with me, I'd have let him take me home and give me cock, hard. I told him that I loved my girlfriend, my cunt was reserved for her, but he could fuck my arse. The guy's dick was practically writhing to get out of his pants. For good measure, I even put my hand on it when no one was looking, before I wiggled sexily back to the protective side of Clare. She played her part really well. When I sat down she got hold of my arm and pinched the skin underneath really hard and called me a slut and said that I was a dirty girl and asked if I was wet. I was. I liked doing it. It was fun. And that's how it went.

One night we were talking to some lads in The Havana, and they steered the subject round to lesbianism (very original). Clare, who hadn't been saying much, suddenly just bent over and kissed me full on the lips. All the guys were shouting, "Hey!" and, "Get in there girl!" and such like. It didn't phase me, I was becoming used to Clare's little ways.

"So you're dykes then?" one of the boys sneered.

"Yeah of course," Clare replied sharply. "*All* girls are. Like *all* boys are poofs."

That confused them somewhat, but the first speaker kept gamely on.

"So if you're lesbians then, show us some of your lesbian stuff."

"What, here?" asked Clare.

"Yeah, here," he said, "I dare you."

Clare looked me solemnly in the eye, "It's a dare Rosie!"

I knew something was gonna happen now but even I wasn't quite ready for what Clare did next. She slumped back in her seat, pulled up her skirt, took hold of my hand and slipped it down the front of her panties. I could feel her soft pubic hair brushing against the palm of my hand

and I was phased, let alone the boys opposite. But Clare just kept going. She singled out one of my fingers and ran it down the groove between her pussy lips and right inside the entrance of her hole. I remember being surprised how wet it was. Then, she withdrew my hand, brought it up to my own mouth and put the finger with her juice on my lips.

"Suck then . . " she said, smiling seductively, and I was so surprised, I did. Well that really knocked the boys out. Their eyes were like saucers and they stared at us without a word, while my tongue lapped at the salty sour cum smeared on my fingertip. I think I was as much in shock as the lads, but I enjoyed the expressions on their faces as I tasted another girl for the first time. Straight away Clare said brightly, "Okay, your turn, one of you has got to feel another's dick. I dare you. I'll fuck whoever does it."

Well you can imagine the reaction. Embarrassed guffaws, sniggers, protests, jokes. Of course, what none of those lads realised was that Clare was deadly serious. If one of them had taken on Clare's challenge and touched a dick he could've had her then and there, or at least out back in the car park. But, time-wasters and cowards to a boy, they missed their chance. Typical.

Another time, was when we were sunbathing in the Cathedral grounds, in our skimpy little tops and shorts, and talking about sex, of course. Clare asked me how I made myself come. Just as I was shyly trying to explain, she interrupted and said, "Show me then!"

"No way!" I said. But she just replied, "Dare you to."
What could I do? I went with her into the bushes and
undid my shorts, slipping them down to my knees. Kneeling, I slid my hand down the front of my blue cotton panties and rubbed. I was a bit nervous, but Clare promised to
keep an eye out, though she seemed to spend most of her
time watching me closely. It wasn't the greatest orgasm
of my life but I got there, and Clare said afterwards she
respected me for taking the challenge.

Not all the dares were about sex. Some were about
shoplifting or stupid things like adding salt to your drinking chocolate. We prided ourselves on our daredevilry and
it could get quite competitive. The thing is, you couldn't
refuse without losing a lot of face. The first time I balked
at a dare was one night when we were having a drink
back at Clare's and she started talking about the time with
the boys in The Havana. She said to me, "You know when
you fingered my pussy?" and I said "Yeah?" and she said
"Well, would you like to lick it?" I just giggled but Clare
slipped her panties off and opened her legs and said
"You've already licked my juice so what's the problem?"
I didn't know what the problem was. I was lying on my
stomach on the floor, staring into my best friend's cunt.
I'd never seen one except for my own. It looked very familiar but strange at the same time. Clare separated her
lips and showed me her clit. She started sliding her fingertip over it and talking at the same time. She was moving her hips now and slipping towards me on the carpet
till she was only about a foot from my face, still talking.

"Why don't you kiss it if you want to? I want you to." I was almost hypnotised. Almost, but something stopped me. This didn't feel like the normal game. I knew she was going to dare me, but as she hadn't actually said it yet, I got in first. "Make yourself come, I dare you." Clare lay back on the floor and started to move her finger really fast over her clitoris. Within a minute, her feet were lifting off the floor and her red lips were completely exposed to my gaze. I watched the moisture form at the entrance to her cunt which had opened so I could see all the folds of rose pink flesh inside. Her juice was running down the crack in her cheeks towards her tight little arsehole. I *was* hypnotised now. When Clare came, I watched her vagina pulsate maybe seven or eight times as the muscles tightened and relaxed. She lay there for a long while before anything was said. I thought she'd be annoyed with me for bottling out. I felt awkward as if I'd let her down, so I made an excuse and went home soon afterwards. But I couldn't get the image of Clare out of my mind as I lay in bed that night masturbating myself to sleep.

That's when things started to change, though I didn't realise it at the time. We'd been shopping and I'd seen this beautiful top. Skin tight but stretchy, because it was made of a really fine mesh that looked as if it was painted on you. It was way too expensive for me and I had said I would do anything for it. Clare had given me that look she has and said, "Anything?" I was waiting for the dare. I expected to have to steal something, or do something dirty involving one of the shop assistants, whatever. She once dared me to strip off in a changing cubicle with the curtain not properly closed so a man standing outside had a view of me. The guy just couldn't believe his luck, especially when it came to the second part, when I had to touch my toes for ten seconds with my back to him. Clare said I looked really dirty from behind and my pussy lips were peeking out very prettily between my thighs. The man went white with fear and excitement. It was a good dare and I enjoyed doing it and wouldn't even mind doing it again. So I kept eyeing up the staff and the clientele, wondering which one Clare would choose, but nothing happened.

We left the shop and after a couple of hours I'd forgotten all about it and we headed back home. As we walked along swinging our shopping, a car slowed down and crawled along next to us. This was nothing unusual, we lived near the red light district. The driver's window opened and Clare leaned into it. I expected her to give the guy the usual earful but she came out with a cheery, "Looking for business mate?" Clare turned to me grinning. For once, I was shocked. She must have seen it in my face because she had this kind of triumphant look all over her. "You said, anything! Okay, fifty quid says you won't give him a hand job." I froze. The man was getting impatient. "Well?" I shook my head. Clare rolled her eyes at me and got into the car which pulled into a back street used for this kind of work. I waited for her on the street corner, giving hard stares at every man who so much as glanced at me. Fifteen minutes later she was back looking extremely smug. "Oh, and you owe me fifty," was all she said. I was annoyed with her. It felt like she'd cheated. I mean a sex dare for money is different. It's changing the rules. I tried to explain this to her but Clare simply said that I'd lost my nerve. I was a prude and I couldn't admit it to myself. I couldn't find the right words to argue with her but I felt, somehow, my bluff had been called.

I avoided her for a couple of weeks after that. Eventually she phoned me, saying she wanted to see me. She had a new boyfriend, Steven, and she wanted me to meet him. I felt strangely annoyed at her. It was like sneaky for her to get involved with a man just because we weren't speaking for a while. A short fling would be okay, but a boyfriend, a regular boyfriend? I was a bit off with her and said I might go round, and Clare said, "Well don't bother if you don't want to," and nearly put the phone down on me. But I figured this would be my opportunity to have my say. Besides I hadn't forgotten the fifty and I didn't want her going round telling everyone that I welshed on my debts.

She opened the front door and walked up the stairs ahead of me without saying a word. I assumed she was still mad at me. When I reached the first floor landing, where her flat was, she turned to me and put a finger up to her lips. "Shh, Rosie. Don't talk, I want to show you something." I just shrugged. Clare was like this, setting little tests to see how you'd react. She beckoned with her finger and I followed her into the flat. She led me through to her bedroom. Stretched out on the bed was a naked man.

He was trussed up by a mass of thin rope that was cutting into his flesh, and his head was covered with a full face mask that blindfolded and gagged him.

I couldn't help noticing he was circumcised and had a cock ring round the base of his prick. I couldn't help noticing because he had a hugely swollen purplish erection launching out of a mass of dark curly hair and up towards the ceiling. I could see Clare watching me, so I tried to look casual. Truth was, the moment I'd seen him lying there, I'd felt an electric tingle in my tummy.

Clare suppressed a giggle and mouthed, "That's Steven!" She grabbed my hand and pulled me back into the living room. "Look Rosie. Don't make any noise, you'll give the game away," she whispered in my ear. I raised my eyebrows. Like, what game? She explained in a hoarse whisper that Steven had asked to have sex like this but she wanted me to do the sex instead of her. She wanted to be girlfriends again, she wanted nothing coming between us. So she wanted to share her boyfriend. It was a secret present to me. It would be our little secret - just her and me. I nodded and Clare said, "If you don't speak and I do, if he only hears my voice, he's gonna assume it's me."

For the second time in our relationship, Clare had that smugly triumphant look on her face that I saw by the kerb-crawler's car.

Behind the door, the trussed-up figure let out a muffled moan. "I'm just coming!" called Clare giggling. Clare winked at me and went into the bedroom, leaving the door ajar. She placed a finger over her lips and padded over to the bed. She bent down, the whole time looking me in the eye and licked the length of Steven's cock till he squirmed and thrust beneath the cords. She looked at me saying "Now, now Steven, don't be hasty or you won't get what I promised you." Steven groaned some more but stopped bucking. Clare returned to my side and pushed me out of the bedroom. Then she grabbed me and kissed me hard, forcing her tongue into my mouth. When she pulled away she was grinning. "What?" I whispered. "You could at least suck his dick," she smirked "I mean my tongue's been up every one of his orifices and *you've* just had it in your mouth!"

Well, yet again I couldn't fault Clare's logic. And I wasn't going to give her the opportunity of calling me a prude again. Besides, there was Steven and the sight of him all bound and helpless was making my pussy wet. Clare snuggled into me and began pinching my nipples. They were already hard and tender and this hadn't escaped her notice. "See, you know you want to, you little slut, you just don't want to admit it."

Thing was, I did want to. But I wasn't going to let Clare use me in her little game with Steven. It would feel too much like she had won. Again, I shook my head. Clare's hand slipped up my skirt and she began running a finger along the gusset of my panties. Then she let the bedroom door swing open and closed so that I got another view of Steven's cock. I couldn't stop the sight of Steven lying on the other side of the door with a great big

27

erection making my cunt muscles contract. Clare must have felt it because her fingers slipped inside the material and my legs nearly buckled as she squeezed my pussy lips together. I had a yearning ache for some action down there now but I couldn't let Clare win so easily. A desperate last ditch compromise with my pride came to me.

"The fifty quid," I whispered. Clare leaned in close to me till I could feel her own hot breath on my ear.

"Do this babe, and all debts will be cancelled," she said. Then came the clincher. "Cos it's a dare!"

I nodded and let Clare slide my panties off, while I wriggled out of my T-shirt. When I took my bra off I realised one of the shortfalls of Clare's planning. My breasts are full and heavy and hers are small and pert. I pointed at my tits then at hers and raised an eyebrow. Clare whispered, "His hands are tied to the bed, he can't lift them up. If you just sit on top of him . . ."

Clare took my hand and led me through to the bedroom again. I climbed onto the bed, got astride Steven and lowered myself onto his erection.

"Ooh that feels good!" oozed Clare sexily.

My pussy was soaking wet by now and I assumed I'd just swallow Steven up without him touching the sides but I was surprised by just how big his cock was. I felt it push into my lips and slip in. I slowly began to rock back and forwards while Clare talked dirty.

"That's it . . . I want your thick, hard cock . . . right in deep. I want it up me. I'm a slut, I love cock up me, ooh yeah, I love it up me. I love to watch it sliding into me. It looks so slutty . . . push it hard."

Her voice kept catching in her throat, like she was getting turned on herself, and the more she talked, the harder I rode Steven, the more he writhed and bucked. I kept thinking, yeah, this was a truly dirty slut-fuck, taking a guy's cock up your cunt in front of his girlfriend, especially as he didn't know it was happening. I was feeling exceptionally horny but I forced myself to slow things down. I had to show Clare I wasn't completely out of control.

I leaned forward on my arms and started to lift my arse off Steven's cock in slow, graceful arcs, taking myself up higher and higher each time, till only the very tip of his penis was still up inside me. Then I'd pause and wait. Judging by the thrashing about on the pillow by the wrapped up head, Steven's need for a pussy grip and his anticipation of it was agony. When I judged the moment was right, I'd suddenly sit right back down on him hard, forcing his pillar of flesh deep into me with a rush and he'd gasp and buckle, whether from pain or pleasure, I couldn't tell. That was the best bit.

I could understand why Clare wanted this. I looked around for her, to see if we could share it, like we were proper girlfriends once again. She'd stopped talking at Steven by now, and was right there kneeling beside me, her eyes glowing with excitement. She started to kiss my shoulder gently. Then I felt her hand stroke my back and between my buttocks till she had a finger either side of my pussy lips, pushing against them and feeling her boyfriend's cock slowly going in and out of me. She leaned towards me and whispered frantically in my ear, "Go on then, slut. Fuck him hard!"

Well that did it for me. I did lose control. I bounced and banged and slid up and down on Steven's hard cock while Clare fingered and explored every slippy little orifice she could find. When her finger went up my cunt with Steven's cock, I orgasmed, shaking and rocking till I collapsed exhausted.

I rolled off Steven's cock. There was thick droplets of cum oozing from the tip. He'd come and I hadn't noticed. When Clare released the cock ring, more of his sperm flooded out. I was lying exhausted on the bed, trying to get my energy back before Clare told me to leave. But she didn't. Then she started releasing Steven from his bonds. Next thing she was unfastening his hood. I stared at her. Wasn't this ruining the game? Clare just smiled her beatific, innocent smile. When Steven's face was revealed, I looked at him astonished. It was the man from the car. Was Clare going out with a kerb-crawler now? I couldn't understand.

After a few pleasantries, the guy, who she called, 'Bill', got dressed and went into the living room. I could hear a bit of muttering, then 'Bill', stuck his head round the corner and said, "Thanks, bye now." And I heard the flat door slam.

I wobbled unsteadily into the living room, naked and perplexed. Clare was stuffing something into her handbag. "Okay, let's go!" she said briskly.

"What, now?" I asked.

"*Now!*" she replied.

I knew Clare was deliberately and provocatively trying to avoid discussing what had just happened. But I thought, this time I won't be the first to crack. So I pulled my clothes on without even showering and followed Clare down the stairs and back outside. She flagged a taxi and took me downtown. We went straight to the store where I'd seen the top and she bought it for me, cash. Then she bought some nice tasty tit-bits from the deli next door and a couple of bottles of wine (not cheap) and we went back to her flat.

While Clare prepared the food she told me to take a shower. I just obeyed. When I was drying myself off she came in and told me to put the top on, she wanted to see me in it. She gave me the top and a sexy little thong she'd bought as well. This was all the clean clothes I had to wear, but the flat was warm, so I wasn't bothered. We gorged ourselves on the food and got tipsy on the wine. Eventually I could keep it in no longer.

"Clare," I said, "about Steven?"

Clare was just taking the lid from a tub of chocolate ice cream and was licking it. She licked her lips and said, "Who's Steven?"

I took a deep breath. "Steven, your boyfriend, who I just fucked. Remember?"

Clare didn't look at me, she just poked her finger in the tub and licked it. "Come on Rosie, stop playing the innocent. You knew there was no Steven. You wanted to fuck that guy in front of me because you're a dirty little slut." She looked up, eyes all a glitter now. "Well?" She challenged.

I wasn't going to argue. Firstly, there was more than a grain of truth in what she said. Secondly, this wasn't the time for an argument, we'd only just got back to being friends. I thought I'd better cool it so I decided on a diversion. I started to giggle.

"What?" She asked. I lay flat on the couch, laughing. Clare cottoned on immediately. "I'm coming Steven, I'm coming!" she panted and jumped astride me, squashing me into the cushions and laughing. Then she started running her hands all over my body going, "You dirty little tart! You whore, you slut!" I looked up at her. She was smiling at me while her nails scratched lightly backwards and forwards across my nipples, pushing against the net of my new top, I felt little tingles zoom all the way down to my stomach. Next thing, her fingers were stroking my belly and, without really thinking much about it, I gave out a little sigh of appreciation. Then, she rolled beside me and kissed me. She smooched me. The bottom just fell right out of my tummy and I yielded to those sexy smooches and snogged her right back. And all the time her hands were running up and down my body. She started kissing my neck and round my breasts, finally concentrating on my nipples, tender and hard against the crisscross mesh. Then, she pulled at the net with her teeth and bit a little hole in it right above one of my trapped nipples. Straight away, the nipple blossomed up through the tear.

But the gap in the material was tight and restricting and the fine strands of mesh cut fiercely into my tender flesh. It was on the line between pain and pleasure. Immediately, Clare started to tease me by flicking her tongue gently over it. This time the tingle went straight to my pussy and my body must have wriggled slightly, because she ran her hand quickly over my tummy and dived right into my thong. She parted my hairs very carefully and slipped a finger between my pussy lips. As she ran her fingertip round the edge of my cunt, I realised how incredibly wet I was. Clare pulled my thong off and tossed it aside. I lay there completely naked on her couch with my legs as wide apart as I could get them while Clare slipped two fingers in and out of my juicy wet hole.

We lay like this for quite a while, Clare teasing and stretching me, all the time whispering things in my ear, telling me what a filthy, dirty girl I was, and asking me if I liked being a whore, and I kept saying, "Yes," very softly and urgently. I was starting up a nice rhythmic response to Clare's fingering when she jumped up and stripped herself naked as quickly as she could, throwing clothing around the flat like frisbees. Then she started rummaging around in a drawer. I was starting to feel abandoned and perplexed. I watched the tight little globes of her arse bob about in front of me while she began fitting something like a suspender belt round her waist. I couldn't figure out what Clare was up to. After a few seconds I found out. She suddenly stood up and turned to face me, a hard rubbery eight inch strap-on sticking out from her lithe curves. I looked at her. She just raised an eyebrow triumphantly, letting the question hang there between us in silence. I tried to answer but I couldn't.

A confused jumble of thoughts tumbled through my mind - like Clare's a girl; like my cunt is really, really wet. I'm not a dyke, honest, but when I looked at Clare I thought, God I need some fucking. It was like Clare had read my mind 'cos she asked, "Yes?" But she needn't have asked and she knew it. My mouth was dry and I couldn't swallow properly so I just rasped, "Please," and swivelled my arse so it was hanging over the edge of the couch.

Clare knelt in front of me and eased the big dildo into me. It went in, in one go, without any resistance. Then, she began to rock back and forth while her right hand stroked and rubbed my pubic hair. The rubber strap-on was going in right to the hilt and I could feel Clare start to really slam in against my open pussy. I think I felt about as dirty as I ever have in my entire life. I'd lifted my legs right up in the air and before I knew it, Clare had the tip of her finger up my arsehole and I was bucking my hips and coming very loudly. It just happened in seconds. Clare was grinning like a Cheshire cat.

"Told you, you were a dirty little slut," she said, and wriggled out of the strap-on harness (which by now had a glistening damp patch around the open gusset). Then she lay next to me on the couch.

"My pussy's really hungry," she said, and took my hand in hers, pushing it down between her legs. My index finger at the entrance of her cunt, just like in front of the boys in the Havana. When it had picked up some of her moisture, she started slowly circling it round her clit, which was all plumped up. Clare looked at me with her eyes wide.

"Do me!" she said.

"I'm not sure how," I said.

"You're a whore aren't you? You'd better learn."

So Clare laid back and began to play with herself, while I again had the pleasure of watching her. She built herself up to a really vigorous rocking rhythm, her knees curled right up while she rubbed and pinched at her clit like a girl possessed.

Then, she suddenly stopped and rolled over.

"C'mon, whore, you know what to do," she growled.

She took my hand and guided it till three of my fingers disappeared inside her, swallowed up by her hot wetness. Her neat girly arse started pumping furiously and she was soon panting like a wild animal. I was shocked and excited to see a girl so desperate for it.

"Kiss my tits," she gasped, and yanked my head up roughly till her full pink nipple was forced between my lips. I sucked and licked it a bit.

"Bite me, whore. Hard!" she snarled, pushing her tit into my mouth.

I pulled her erect nipple between my teeth and nipped it sharply, sucking and biting till she came, wriggling and bucking, and her cum oozed out over my hand and ran down my arm.

Eventually, she lay back purring like a cat and grinning all over her face.

"Thank you, you tart, you'll be rewarded."

And that's how it started, our little game. Clare picks up the punters and deals with the administrative side, then she tells me what I've got to do. We don't bother with the daring bit anymore, that's understood. I do the business, while Clare watches. I fuck men, I fuck women. I fuck anything. Always, Clare's right next to me, whispering dirty little insults in my ear. She tells me what I am, a whore, a slut, a tart. I love to hear her say it. I always give value for money, because that's what Clare wants me to do. Our punters always leave satisfied. And afterwards, we just soft-fuck each other, slowly, for a nice long while, till Clare's ready, and then I do whatever she wants done to her. Sometimes I lick her. Sometimes, I wear the strap-on. I do anything she wants. I can't say no to her. I'll really do anything for her. I'm probably in love with her. I'm definitely in love with being a slut.

Bettina writes,

*If you've ever had the hots for someone
then you'll know how this girl feels.
This passionate recipe made me burn
with a hot desire and a hunger to be satisfied
- but can you have your cake and eat it . . .*

The Burning Within

THE BURNING WITHIN

I met him about a month before it happened.

He was tall, dark, and all the rest of it. He made me tingle when I thought about him. I'd lay in bed at night thinking about him, and fantasize about him making love to me gently. I'd dream about him taking me hard in all kinds of positions. Backwards, forwards, upside-down. Every way I could imagine. I wished my mind would take me further than this. Make me feel his size, his strength and his touch.

I'm not the most sexually experienced person I know, but I've had a few encounters, most of which are not amazingly exciting. Excitement was what I craved and I knew I had a good chance of having this guy deliver.

My dreams were overrun with this man who was everything I thought I needed. I would wake in the night from a dream of him and engage in making love to myself. I'd find myself forcing my hand between my legs, pretending it was him. Pushing three fingers inside my pussy, pretending it was him. Bringing myself to orgasm with his hands, his cock filling me. Once relaxed again, I'd slip into a dream-like state where I would feel myself sleeping in his arms, completely satisfied.

That weekend, the fifth weekend after we'd met, I

had decided that I would give in to his charms. My imagination was not doing me justice. My frantic masturbation sessions were not delivering the satisfactory goods.

He arrived at my house at nine o'clock, and he looked as sexy and well turned out as usual. He smelt of shower gel mixed with aftershave and I nearly disrobed that second. I could feel my pussy getting hot and wet and needed a moment in my bathroom before leaving.

He had booked a table at the Ricky Loder Restaurant Bar, which was extremely expensive and high profile. Although impressive, the venue did not match up to the company. He was truly the best looking man I had ever set my eyes on. He was a man of few words, yet I felt as if he had told me everything.

The first time he'd kissed me had felt too intense. I was afraid of his control, and I knew he would be hard to resist but I had managed to hold off. Now the excitement of giving in to him was almost too much for me.

I ate dinner without tasting it, my mind more wrapped up in deciding how he would feel against me, and what he would want to do to me later.

My body throbbed in anticipation, my hand slipped downwards to my lap so many times through dinner that I was considering a trip to the ladies to relieve my tensions. No, that would make tonight less special. I wanted him to get me there, not my hot little hand.

I felt him brush the inside of my leg. He had slipped his shoe off and was stretching his foot up towards my hottest part. I throbbed with desire and had to hold my breath to stop myself from crying out. I'd never been so desperate for a man to make love to me and I almost felt ashamed of my need. His foot slid up my inner thigh and found the bare skin at the top of my stockings. He explored between my legs with his probing toes. I put down my fork and closed my eyes.

"I'm going to put myself inside you soon," he said, and I opened my eyes in shock. He looked at me casually and I couldn't tell if I had imagined those words. My heart thumped and I shook from the pit of my stomach.

After dinner he led me to his car and opened the door for me. I realised I couldn't remember one conversation we had spoken about, and so I struggled with the related subjects. I didn't care. We drove to the junction where he always stops. One way my apartment, one way his.

"Let's go your way shall we?" I heard myself saying, disembodied.

"Fine," came the deep-voiced reply.

I had held out to his tactics for over a month and it had been a real struggle. Our dates had always ended with a kiss goodnight outside my front door.

I was finding it hard to breathe, my chest was constricted and my heart thumped noisily. I wasn't sure if my legs would carry me when we arrived. My head issued images of him scooping me up and lifting me straight to his bedroom which would be white; white bed, white carpets, white sheets.

My daydreaming was interrupted when we pulled into a dark driveway. A very long dark driveway. It was pretty rural out here and very secluded. Up ahead I could see a huge house. Huge, that word suited him. Huge personality, huge car, huge house. I hoped he was consistent.

"You live here?"

He nodded and flashed me his diamond smile, which immediately put me at ease. I could imagine how many women that smile had put at ease, and I wondered how long the list was to which my name was soon to be added.

The house was incredible, it was like one of the country manor houses you'd see in a Miss Marple murder case. I smiled at the thought of drinking 'brandy in the drawing room'.

We entered the house. The hall was bigger than my flat. He took my coat. I was wearing the most expensive and revealing dress I had ever bought. This past five weeks had cost me a fortune. Buying new make-up and expensive outfits to match his designer suits and expensive restaurants. The lingerie I was wearing had cost me £150, but when I saw it I just had to have it. It was so beautiful, lilac satin trimmed with lace and fine ribbon, not the sort of thing I'd usually wear, but his man was special. Let's hope he lives up to his image, I thought, and then scolded myself for being so shallow.

He took me by the hand and led me to the next room. It was beautiful. It had a high ceiling with a rose in the centre, a very ornate fireplace, and a couple of deep velvet sofas.

He stood behind me as I admired the room. I could feel his eyes burning into me. He was close behind me.

His hands on my hips. His lips close to my neck. He towered above me, a good twelve inches above, and hopefully . . .

The lights were dim, and were already on when we arrived and I wondered if he left them like this each time we had met, just in case.

All these questions would be answered in time.

He spun me around and I caught my breath just before he closed his mouth over mine.

I pulled away playfully. "Don't I even get a drink?" I asked trying to look and sound seductive.

He shook his head. "Afterwards," he muttered, not taking his eyes from me as he led me through into the bedroom.

I was melting. Who wanted a drink anyway, not me, I was about to get high from this man's body.

He pulled me back. Smothering me in tingling kisses and light caress. He unzipped my glittering blue dress and slid his hands down my back. He sighed in my ear.

I was drowning . . remember to breathe . . . remember to breathe . . . I chanted in my mind.

He was consuming me. He seemed ten foot tall and growing in all directions. He slipped off my dress; down it fell to the floor. I stood in my lilac underwear and high-heels. My chest bounced with my heart beat and my breasts were firm with erect nipples. I had never felt so sexy and wanted.

My mind wondered ahead, thinking of him pounding into me. I shook off the thought and tried to concentrate on the moment at hand.

He pulled my hand down to his belt. I undid it, fumbling with excitement. He pulled off his trousers, and tugged his shirt over his head. He rubbed his whole body against me and engulfed me. I felt myself disappear inside him as he covered me with his arms and curled them round me. He lifted me to the bed which was nearly three times the size of mine. He stood back and eased down his underwear as he stared into my eyes. I felt as if I would explode. He lived up to my fantasies. His whole body was perfect and I couldn't believe my luck.

"Take them off." He commanded. I wasn't going to argue.

I reached behind me and flicked the clasp off of my bra, first time. Everything was going right. I wriggled my panties down and he stared between my legs. He walked round to the end of the bed and looked down at me.

"Open for me." Not a question, an order. I gulped, but obeyed. Slowly I opened up for him and laid my legs wide for him to see me.

He breathed heavily. The head of his penis glistened. My middle burned with desire and need for him.

He bent down and moved on the bed, slowly crawled up until his arms were between my legs. Never taking his eyes from mine. He spread me out as far as possible. Self-consciousness left me as I realised how excited he was.

He pushed out his tongue and slowly lowered his head. He touched his tongue to my clitoris and slowly circled it. I moaned out loud and burned within. His tongue pushed and flickered. His hand moved up and his fingers teased me. I pushed down.

"Don't move," he said firmly.

He wanted to control me and I was enjoying it. He entered me with his tongue and fingers. I was in heaven, yet scared to move. Being scared was new to me, but it was adding to the feelings.

He stopped and stood. His hand moved to his erection, which was straining. He moved around the bed and offered himself to my face. I lifted my head and licked the tip. He thrust himself into my mouth, and held my head still as he entered and pulled out over and over again. I gasped for air. He tasted fresh and clean.

"Touch yourself," he gasped and I immediately pushed my hands between my legs.

"In a moment, I'm going to take your pussy," he said, staring down at me. He pulled out of my mouth. "Is that what you want?" He knew it was. I nodded. "Say it."

"I want you inside me," I whispered.

He put his face to mine.

"When?"

I was dying for it. "Now!"

He smiled and licked my lips.

He returned to the end of the bed and knelt between my legs. He twisted me over so I laid on my front. He pulled me to my knees and lifted my buttocks up, until I knelt with my chest on the bed. His stomach pushed against my arse and the tip of his length was against my clit. He rubbed it with himself and lifted himself to tease my opening.

"Do it . . ." I didn't finish.

He eased in and I have never been so filled.

He was taking me slowly. I was facing a mirror. I lifted up and stared at myself being fucked by this man who was controlling my every move. Pushing into me, fucking me, filling me. He stared into my eyes in the mirror and grasped me hard. Pushing deep into me, faster and faster. Harder and harder. I found it hard to breathe. His hand on my breast, squeezing my tender nipple. I exploded. I came hard and fast. It spread through my body, top to bottom.

He continued thrusting, pushing.

He roared and pulled out of me, shooting cum all over my buttocks, back and pussy.

He kissed my back and pulled away. I watched him walk, naked, to the door. He turned, "Get some sleep." He smiled and left the room.

And never came back.

Bettina writes,

Here's an experience that I related to my good friend Shelly, and she was kind enough to use her writing talent to tell it just as hot as it was . . .

A Dream Invitation

A DREAM INVITATION

Visibility was terrible. I could hardly see the road in front of me. I was over half way there and my imagination was running wild. Robert was the most amazing man. I had only spent a short amount of time with him, and so the invitation had really come out of the blue. I didn't even realise he knew where I lived, but he had found out somehow and I was glad. I knew he was the sexiest man I had ever encountered and the thought of him touching me took my breath away. 'Saturday at 9' the invitation said, 'I have something for you at my house - you'll love it. Robert'. Sounded mysterious.

So tonight was the night. I was driving to the address on the invitation. I knew I was going there to give myself to a man I hardly knew. I could feel the wetness between my legs soiling the new underwear I had bought for him to take off.

As I drove up the wide drive, the house seemed empty. Darkness surrounded me and the rain cooled down my mood. The door was already open and I entered. The house was massive, it must have contained twenty rooms which all appeared to be in darkness. My mouth was slightly open as I breathed heavily. I took a few steps, and on the floor was an envelope with my name on it. I opened it.

'Slip off your clothes'. The words were typed and small on a large piece of paper. I took a deep breath. Should I cut my losses and run back into the stormy night, or join in with these sexy games. The thought of Rob pounding inside me flashed through my mind and my pussy ached with desire. I closed my eyes and removed my coat and let it fall to the floor. I took off my top, pulled down my skirt and stepped out of it. I was aroused to the point where I thought I would lay on the floor here and touch myself until I exploded.

I heard a noise. I was standing in a dark hallway in my black bra and skimpy knickers. I could hear groaning coming from the room nearest me. A dim light was turned on.

"Come in. Please come in here," a faint voice beckoned me. I slowly opened the door and what I saw embarrassed and turned me on incredibly. A man with a beautiful body holding the legs of a beautiful woman. They were naked and looked at me as I stood in the doorway. His erection was straining.

"Fuck me Angel," said the blonde haired woman whose legs were spread as she waited for him to fill her. I froze at the sight before me.

"Come here," the man said to me. I walked towards him automatically resigned to whatever the evening may hold. The woman writhed almost in pain trying to pull him into her. I stood beside them and looked at his throbbing penis.

"Touch it," he hissed at me. Nervously I touched it.

He exhaled and threw back his head. He took my hand and pulled me behind him. I cupped his testicles as he knelt between her legs. My breasts bounced as I breathed and I could feel sweat breaking on my forehead. Slowly he moved forward and touched the head of his cock to the entrance of the woman's pussy. Her eyes were closed and her arms were back as he sank it into her, pushing his cock as far as he could.

"Oh," I gasped as I felt a rush of fresh juice between my thighs. His face was screwed up as my hand held his balls and his cock was swallowed by her beautiful pussy. He moved inside her and I watched with fascination as he disappeared into her.

"Touch me," she said, and as I looked her eyes were staring at me and I realised she meant me. "Please?" she begged. I reached to her and teased her wet clitoris as his cock fucked her. I was holding two strangers as they fucked. Where was Rob? My imagination brought him to me, and I imagined him helping himself to my rear, thrusting his hard cock into my wide open pussy as I fondled these people. Being fucked from behind, having his cock enter me, needing him to slam himself into my aching pussy.

The man gasped as he slipped in and out, in and out. The woman pushed herself hard on to him. Her naked breasts bounced and I fingered her opening as the large cock moved in and out. As he came, he withdrew and sprayed my hand, and her pussy with warm cum. The woman still writhed around and I knew she had been on the edge of her own orgasm. Her frustration was obvious. The man got up and wiped himself down.

The door opened behind me and another man entered wearing just black silk pyjama bottoms. Without a word he replaced the other man inside her. He pulled down his trousers and put himself inside her without even noticing me. He seemed oblivious, he knew what he wanted and took it. How long had he been there? How long had he been watching us?

I backed out of the room. I felt shocked and bursting with sexual energy. I walked along the corridor aware of the cool breeze on my erect nipples. As I tip-toed slowly along I slipped a finger into my knickers and further, into my sopping wet pussy. Wonderful sensations washed over my body. Pulling my knickers down, I gently touched my clitoris and shuddered.

Suddenly I became aware I was being watched. I turned around and saw a tall man. He was wearing a black suit and tie and looked as though he had just come from a dinner party, and here I was standing in my underwear playing with myself. He was extremely good looking and at least six foot tall. He smiled down at me and touched my cheek.

"Come," he said, and I did.

I followed him into a room, which was as bare as I was. A huge rug covered the mahogany coloured wooden floor, and six candles lit the room. Slightly alarmed by the experience I had just encountered, my legs began to wobble and I needed to sit.

"Here." He took my hand and he knelt on the floor. I knelt in front of him. He smelt amazing and I could feel his breath on my moist cheeks. He removed his coat and started unbuttoning his shirt. A tattoo on his arm read 'Allan'.

"I'm here to see Rob," I said nervously.

"Rob will be here soon, he asked me to entertain you."

The hairs on the back of my neck stood up. I looked between his legs, and could see his large erection trying to escape from his trousers. He ran the back of his hand down my breast and lightly pulled at my bra, exposing my nipple.

"Rob will . . ." I began but he finished with:

"Rob won't mind. Relax."

His chest was hard and toned and his face wore a permanent smile. I was drowning in sexual tension. He guided my hand to my own centre and I felt the moist material between my legs. Gently he pushed me backwards. I sat upright on the floor and he pulled at my knickers until they slipped down my long legs. He parted my legs as I sat. He stared at me, and I could feel my cheeks flushing red hot.

"You're beautiful," he said. He moved towards me and brushed his hand up my inner thigh, stopping short of what he knew I wanted. I lent back on my arms, legs still wide. He lowered his head to me and licked up and down my thighs. My breath was hard to find and my nipples were hard as rocks. His tongue teased around me and I nearly begged him to lick my pussy. I gasped as the tip of his tongue circled my clitoris. I threw back my head in ecstasy as he slipped a long finger into my dripping pussy.

"Emmm", he groaned as two fingers probed my hole and his tongue sucked at me. He pulled off his trousers with his free hand. He stood in front of me. His large penis in front of me, throbbing at me. He held my head and pressed his cock to my lips. I opened my mouth obediently and tasted his cock on my tongue. I sucked his cock as he moved his powerful hips back and forth, forcing his cock between my lips.

My thoughts arrived at Rob again, he was becoming a blur. I couldn't remember how he looked. This man was overtaking my thoughts. He was just amazing to look at, and here he was with his cock slipping in and out of my mouth, and I nearly choked as I thought of his cock fucking my pussy hard. My hand travelled to my pussy and I used my fingers to stimulate myself. I looked up at him. His eyes glared as I fucked myself with my fingers. He withdrew suddenly. I continued to work on my pussy, harder and harder, shamelessly. He watched with wide, eager eyes. He lowered himself and grabbed my hips. I fell backwards and he caught my head as I fell. His powerful hips were between my legs, and I could feel the tip of his cock on my leg. He flipped me over masterfully and pulled me back, and I groaned with anticipation at what he was about to do to me. I looked up at the reflection we made in the patio doors. He sat back on his heels and pulled my legs either side of him, my pussy wide and open, ready for his cock. I lay on my stomach with my bottom sticking up, feeling his cock searching for my entrance.

The headlights of a car came up along the driveway and shone through the patio doors. Someone got out and approached, looking down at me. Allan found his goal. I buckled as he eased his large cock into my burning hot pussy.

"Oh yes," he groaned as he widened my opening and sunk deep, deep inside me. The man at the window was watching. I could feel him. I gave in to this strange situation, not caring that I was being watched, needing this man to fuck me, fuck me. I raised my head and looked at the man outside who smiled at me. He was leaning on the glass. I looked at his face. Rob! It was Rob, and he was watching me being fucked by another man. I felt my end coming. I felt a volcano building inside me. I was aching from the pit of my stomach. I screamed out, I couldn't control it. I stared at Rob as I left this world for a second. Rob mouthed the word over and over, ' . . . beautiful! . . . beautiful!' Allan slammed into me as he exploded, filling my pussy with cum. I could feel it oozing out of me around his cock. He was pumping into me. I looked up, Rob was gone.

I lay back on the warm rug. Allan kissed my cheek and left the room. I was alone again. I dressed quickly, I couldn't face Rob now. How could I?

I left the house and drove home. I was in shock. Did this evening really happen? How could I have let it happen? I could feel Allan's juices inside me, I guess it did happen!

I arrived home. The answer machine was flashing. I pressed play to hear the message. It was Rob: 'Hi! I told you I had something for you at my house, didn't I, I was right that you'd love it. Wasn't I? Well I hope I'll see you soon.'

. . . and then I woke up! I was burning hot and my pussy felt like it had been fucked. It felt so real I wondered if I had been astral dreaming or something. You know where you meet up with other people on an astral plane, and they are dreaming too.

Either way, I hope I get invited back again . . .

. . . Bettina x x x

Bettina writes,

I expect that you'll remember my friend Candy, and if you've read my second book you'll know that she likes being spanked more that anything else. One mention of the word cane, and she gets so wet she has to change her panties. Candy often bends over and begs to be spanked, sometimes I have to help her out myself.

Brace yourself Candy, I put this one in especially for you . . .

The Girl Needs a
Firm Hand

THE GIRL NEEDS A FIRM HAND

She turned to the pile of schoolgirl clothes. White blouse, a short green pleated skirt, white knee socks and old fashioned blue school knickers. She picked up the knickers and smiled as she eased them up her long legs. Designed as they were for a schoolgirl, they were really tight over her distinctly womanly backside. They pulled her buttocks together and bit into her pussy. She slipped on and buttoned up the school blouse; not wearing a bra her aroused nipples were taut against the fabric. Then she pulled on the white knee socks and put on the tiny dark green skirt.

Zipping up the skirt she glanced in the mirror. Her reflection confirmed that she only had to bend over slightly for the half moons of flesh below the line of the knickers to peep out. The tight cotton barely contained her backside, and the knickers crept up slightly every time she moved. She selected a black high-heeled pair of shoes and again inspected herself and the effect these had on her thighs and the jut of her bottom.

"In here please," he called out.

She tottered on her heels down the hallway. As she entered the room he was sitting impassively with a cane across his lap.

"Don't we knock then?"

His voice was harsh, and she felt her glance fall to the

floor.

"Come in then, yes all the way. Turn round."

She did as she was told.

He stood, and placed the cane in a long dark wood case that was open on the table.

"I hope we won't be needing that," he said, closing the lid. He looked her up and down disapprovingly.

"Regulation shoes? I think not. You know what happens to girls who flout the dress code!" And her skirt was whipped up, and a stinging blow from his hand landed on her bottom.

She was shocked by his sudden action and her backside glowed hot.

"Have you any idea what's in this report?" He brandished it, and she turned slightly to see what he had in his hand.

"Did I say turn round? I don't think so."

She stood still. The first imprint of his hand still stung slightly as she waited to hear his next words.

"What about this one from your gym mistress: A lazy girl whose natural talent for gymnastics is totally wasted. Touch your toes and let's see how supple you are ..."

She bent over.

"Oh, natural talent . . . I think you can do better than that." She felt his hand gently push her lower, and she was aware that, with her having bent down so far, the knickers were covering very little.

"Impressive, I can see that you *do* have a gift."

He lifted the tiny skirt and ran his hands up her thighs,

cupping her exposed buttocks for a moment, running one finger in between her legs and over her pussy.

His first strokes were soft, almost caressing. The sensation was not unpleasant. Then, he pulled the material of the knickers up and into the crack, and two strong, stinging blows landed, one on each buttock. She gasped, but was desperate not to cry out.

"Stand up then, and let's have a look." He tucked the skirt into the waistband and pulled the knickers down to frame the full swell of her backside. "I seem to have made an impression already. Does it hurt?"

"Not really." She realised her mistake too late, as two further hard slaps hit her, making her buttocks jiggle.

"But you felt that . . . and these . ." More heavy smacks rained down. Suddenly the stinging turned to pain and she felt sobs well up inside her.

He stopped as suddenly as he'd started.

"Go and stand over there and let's see what else your report reveals."

She stood in the corner facing the wall.

"Perhaps you can give me some good reasons why I shouldn't use the cane next?"

"I try my best in class . . . I do as I'm told . . ."

"You obviously haven't been trying hard enough then, have you, young lady?"

"No."

"No - what?"

"No Sir."

She could hear him pulling the school desk into the

centre of the room.

"Let's try this then."

She turned to come towards him.

"Stay there please. Hands on your head."

She obeyed slowly, and as she raised her arms, her breasts rubbed against the blouse, her nipples erect and extra sensitive. He went to stand behind her. As she stood still the warmth of her bottom was spreading round and infusing her pussy with a total longing to be touched.

After what seemed like an age, she felt his hands once more caressing her bottom cheeks. She shifted her weight a little and opened her legs slightly, and his hands brushed the inside of her thighs. She wriggled to bring her sex in contact with his hand which he withdrew.

"Ah, ah," he tutted, "you're not supposed to be enjoying this you know."

"Let's see." He pulled her by the arm over to the desk and put the report in front of her, bending her over to read it at the same time. By now she was so turned on she felt desperate for some sexual contact. He walked around in front of her, and reached for the long case. He opened it slowly and took out the cane. He flexed the cane and pointed to each subject report, every one worse than the one before. The cane tapped down the list.

"Not very good reading is it? One stroke for each subject don't you think? Well?"

"Yes Sir," she whispered. Her pussy was hot and aching.

"Bend further forward . . . right down over the desk

now, and hold on to the legs." The posture was very demeaning, and she could feel her bottom and thighs stretched over the desk top. The desk had that old familiar schoolroom smell. He swished the cane through the air a couple of times, and she began to wonder just how much it would hurt. But, aching for stimulation as she was she would take anything.

The first thing she felt was him steadying the cane against her bum. He slid it too and fro to establish his aim. Instinctively she clenched her buttocks.

"Nice and relaxed now." He cupped her buttocks with his hands, and measured the cane against her once more. She felt the sting of pain almost before she had heard the swish through the air: this really hurt. She bit her lip, anxious not to cry out. He thrashed her three more times on either side of the first blow, and then paused. The stinging was appalling. But the more the blood rushed to her burning backside, the more she ached for him to take her. He rubbed her, where the cane had brought up slight ridges. The cane came down twice more on the same spot. This time she had to cry out, there was no way she could stop herself, half gasps and sobs now.

"As far as I can see we're only half way down the list here."

"Please no more, it really hurts!"

"Well then, some alternative way must be found for you to make recompense. Perhaps a service that you could perform for me?"

"I'm sure I can Sir . ." She was still over the desk, her

well developed breasts flat against it, staring at the floor. There was a movement behind her, and then, without warning, he thrust himself deep into her pussy from behind. She gasped with the relief of feeling him inside her.

"Harder! Harder!" she cried and he slammed her against the lid with the strength of his onslaught. She grasped the legs of the desk, her knuckles white, the breath nearly being knocked out of her with each thrust. His ejaculation flooded into her causing her to come at the same moment. Arching her back she pushed herself onto him as far as she could, releasing her own frustration. He pulled out and she slumped forward to get her breath back.

"Now go back to your lessons and try to do better in future."

She pulled up her damp knickers and tidied her uniform.

"Put the cane away in it's case before you go."

She picked up the cane and placed it meticulously back in it's case, closing the lid carefully. She put the case into the cupboard and he glanced over to check her actions.

"Ah, that's better," he said, "everything is tidy and as it should be."

Bettina writes,

*I received this story recently and I really
enjoyed reading it. Afterwards I found myself
browsing in those shops where shiny rubber
can be found . . . don't you just love the
tightness of it, the feel of it . . .*

Screen Sex

SCREEN SEX

Carolyn closed her eyes, a smile forming on those full, red-painted lips. She felt the radiant heat permeating through her body; ebony rubber shone new, freshly polished and buffed, close against her naked flesh. The catsuit had been made to order, a size too small for her. It was a squeeze to get on and off - a copious powdering of talc, a significant amount of straining, pulling and stretching. But when it was on, it looked and felt astonishing.

She ignored the incessant buzz, parting her legs, simply allowing the pleasure to capture her senses, to play with her emotions. Her breathing quickened, hollow, ghostly, echoing down the long, narrow tube, through the pack girdling her chest, and back again circuitously, in an endless loop. Her green eyes peered through the mirrored plastic. She could see out, but no one was able to see in.

The television entertained itself, twenty-one inch screen, upon which two half-clad rubber bodies entwined in a mingling congress. But the video played to no-one as Carolyn discovered a pleasure for herself, switching the internally vibrating dildos up another number. There were two of these elongated devices, one in her pussy, the other up her tight arse, and both controlled from one small infrared keypad. Commencing at slow and gradual, the vibrations could be turned up to maximum. Carolyn had a preference for slowly building up to midway, working up to a mind-blowing orgasm. There was no rush. She was certainly in no rush.

She glanced at the screen. The level of her clever stimulators was keeping her on a permanent knifes edge, and she didn't know how long she'd be able to last. Not to the end of the film, but maybe to the scene where he goes down on the girl in a sixty nine, sheathing his cock within the restrictive vacuum of her mouth . . .

Knock, knock!

The buzzing stopped as Carolyn listened, turning her head, her eyes to the patio doors. A face peered through the glass, hands pressing with palms forward, hot breath causing a pool of mist to form on the otherwise clear surface.

Carolyn grabbed the hood, disconnected the hose. She shook her head, releasing auburn locks. She pulled the handle down, and slid the door back on it's metal track with a subdued whoosh. She let in the girl and closed it quickly.

"Hi Amanda! I . . ." Carolyn stumbled over her words. "What must you think of me!"

"Hey don't worry," said Amanda. "We all have our little *eccentricities*. And you do look good in black!"

Carolyn stepped towards the TV and set the tape to rewind.

"Any good?" said Amanda, pointing to the screen.

"Oh, I was just about to put it away, it's not mine, it's

just something someone left here once."

"Let's have a look . . . is it porn? I like to watch porn. Especially if it's two girls together - is there any of that on the tape."

"Well, yes!" stammered Carolyn, "there's all sorts on there."

"Or blow jobs, I really like watching blow jobs on really huge dicks!" said Amanda indicating an appropriately large size with her hands. "I love to see cum dripping from a beautiful girl's lips. Let's put it back on, and we'll watch it together. Here let me find something."

Amanda knelt by the screen and pressed the button on the video machine. Flickering for a few seconds, the picture cleared on to a couple, both young, both good looking, sheathed head to toe in thin black rubber. The girl was a blonde, a true blonde, made obvious by the yawning, unzipped gap between her legs, visible as her lover's tongue slowly lathered the pink slit flossed in a sparse light bush. His head was moving up and down, his mouth sucking the juices onto his tongue. "Oh darling, darling, yes . . . ooh yes!" The blonde reached down to slowly unzip her partner's catsuit, freeing his swelling cock. The head was shiny, almost purple with lust, wet with pre-come. She carefully stroked the shaft, as it pulsed beneath her fingertips, working her hand up and down the strident length.

Amanda was transfixed and slowly she slid her hand down her front, gently caressing her breasts as she watched the screen. Lifting her short cotton skirt, she slipped her fingers inside her red nylon g-string, openly masturbating in front of her friend. Carolyn watched Amanda's fingers inside her g-string, its surface moistening and tight against a sweet scented warmth. Amanda's eyes were closed now, her breathing was heavy, laboured. The film didn't matter any more; her hands were fluttering, spreading, exploring, and her orgasm was closer and closer.

Carolyn pulled the hands away, keen on taking charge. She tore at the blouse - buttons burst, a red nylon bra unclipped. Her prey was soon naked, ready for her to consume. Her shiny rubber pressed against Amanda's smooth naked flesh. She wasted no time in sucking at those tiny pointy nipples, breasts slight, boyish mounds topped with pale pink. Her lips closed around each nipple, tugging, pulling and yanking. She went to one, then to the other, back and forth, licking, sucking, drawing them into her mouth.

"Mmm," came the sigh. Amanda opened her legs further, as far as she was able to let the feminine fingers find her pussy, stroking and caressing. The juice that seeped from Amanda's opening was pure to Carolyn; a single, minute droplet falling from her finger, spiralling onto the floor of her tongue. Carolyn's hot breath ignited an undulating ecstasy, with legs splaying, convulsing.

"Oh, oh yes!" Amanda moaned, her fingers curling, isolating wisps of auburn hair, holding the face to her burning wet breasts, exhorting hungry licks and fastidious devourings. She was not about to let go, not until she had come.

Her body writhed, as if it were under alien direction, with cries and jerks. It was difficult for Carolyn to stay on top of her friend, the bucking was so intense; she shook, and tremors pulled from every direction.

Then Amanda lay still.

"Wow, that was some orgasm you had!" Carolyn exclaimed.

Amanda drew a long, deep breath before answering.

"That was so, so . . . the best ever!"

Carolyn noticed the still stiff apex of nipple and let her nail brush the tip, causing its owner to give a tiny shiver. "I've never seen such a powerful climax," she said, planting a single kiss on the same nipple.

"But then you've never had sex with a woman before have you?" said Amanda.

"No, that's true."

"Or been made love to *by* a woman. . . I think its time for me to take you in hand! Let's have a shower."

Carolyn stood under the shower. Water jetted from the nozzle. It was a power shower, with the strength to swat away the perspiration-pasted talcum powder that stuck to Carolyn's skin.

"Need a hand?" Amanda stepped onto the plastic tray, pressing her small breasts against Carolyn's back and her thighs against Carolyn's thighs. Finding her firm breasts adept fingers tweaked, turning pouting pink nipples into rigid stops. Amanda unhooked the shower pipe from its holder, and pressed it up to Carolyn's cunt lips. The gush of hot water brought a quick response from her clitoris, and she juddered, grabbing hold of the shower rail with her hand to stop herself from falling. Amanda kept the shower spray in position while her other hand pushed it's way into Carolyn's mouth. Carolyn sucked the fingers and shut her eyes as the jets pumped into her like a continuous ejaculation. She was not long in coming, screaming as the orgasm tore its endless way through her arching body.

"Come here." Amanda rubbed hard with the towel and Carolyn's tousled locks dried quite easily. She patted her high-tipped breasts, then encircled her slender waist, moving the towel between Carolyn's parted legs, pressing it against her pussy.

"Mmm," sighed Carolyn as Amanda kissed the inviting delicious pink lips.

The scene changed to the bedroom. Amanda stretched out her arms, a slinky cat slowly unfurling, her head resting against the pillow, gasping as lips came down, feint as they touched her breasts, sucking her nipples.

Carolyn licked, tracking a path down to the smooth, flat belly, to the indented navel, orbiting, round and round, dipping in and out, Amanda moaning, shivering. Carolyn's tongue trailed down to the dark shadow, fingers parting hairs to enable entry to the secret interior. Amanda tightened involuntarily, seemingly overwhelmed by the probing pervasion, learning to relax and relish what was being done to her. She turned her head sideways, the pressing weight, breast to breast, pussy to pussy, the slow, grinding motion, the contact of Carolyn's sex against her own. She wrapped both legs around Carolyn, locking their bodies together, their pussies together, clitoris rubbing against clitoris, the hot friction, burning, pushing up, not content to be the submissive, taking over, delivering the orgasm.

"Look, my pussy is so wet and open," Amanda said looking up.

Slithering from Amanda's sweating, heaving body, Carolyn looked down at her own swollen cunt. It was drenched with love juice, a deep flushing red. It was puffed up and bloated from friction and arousal.

"I need some more, *lots* more!"

Amanda smiled, leaning on one elbow. "That can be arranged!"

In the garage the car gleamed, a brand new, shining black BMW. Amanda closed the door, the door that lead from the house into the garage. Naked, as was Carolyn, she perched on the bonnet of the car, parting her legs, pushing her slit forward.

"Eat my cunt," she said, "stick your tongue right up me and fuck me with it."

Carolyn's eyes widened. She was happy to oblige. Spreading the sticky wet lips with her hands, pushing her tongue inside, driving the tip against anything she could find. Amanda used her hands to stop herself from sliding off the bonnet, bracing herself against the cold metal, groaning as Carolyn's tongue licked inside her.

"Lick harder! Push in! Fuck me!" She panted, cried, groaned and moaned.

Carolyn slipped a hand underneath Amanda's peachy arse, bending a finger to go between her cheeks. She gave one push, didn't care if it hurt, and inserted it as far as she could. Amanda's eyes dilated, she yelled, and came, a flood gushing into Carolyn's mouth, down her chin, onto the car and onto the concrete floor. She kept her lips to Amanda, drinking, she didn't stop, even as the legs, thrashing down on the car, threatened to smack her face.

Carolyn told Amanda to turn on to her tummy, to lie flat against the vehicle, keeping her waiting until she found something. A length of rubber tubing. It was smooth, about half an inch in diameter, and went easily into the lubricated channel. Amanda slid slightly, a few inches down the bonnet, dangling her legs off the end, fluttering her eyelashes, sighing, drawing breath, as Carolyn pushed more and more of the tube inside. Carolyn stopped only when there was no more to hold, when almost ten inches had disappeared into Amanda's cunt. She waited a moment before dislodging half of the tube, sliding that part into her own cunt, prostrating herself upon Amanda's back, pussy to arse. Both women engaging a similar shaft of rubber. Rocking her hips in a hunching motion, she fucked Amanda, at the same time fucking herself. When they came, it was as one with deafening cries and yells bounding off the garage walls.

There were so many things, so many tools they could use, scraps of metal, straps of nylon. Carolyn fastened

Amanda's wrists together and gagged her mouth with a piece of cloth she found in the cars glove compartment. She roped her up, arms raised, suspended from a steel bar, with her feet just touching the ground. She had Amanda at her mercy. What should she do? An intriguing decision.

"You want to come?" Grease covered Carolyn's hands as she dug great globules out of the tin. "I'm going to make you come, darling, on my fist."

She slowly pushed her right hand against Amanda's cunt, inserting her fingers, pushing her hand in up to the wrist. Amanda moaned, unable to resist. Carolyn swivelled her around without withdrawing, pushing two fingers into Amanda's arse, fucking her at both ends. In and out, thrusting deep, slowly, fast. She would make her come, give her a massive orgasm!

Amanda kicked her feet and made muffled sounds, unable to shout or scream with pain or pleasure, stifled by the gag. Carolyn didn't stop fucking her, she just carried on.

"Go girl, fucking go!" The man shouted as hot jets of his cum splashed over his computer screen and keyboard. He hadn't had time to grab the tissue placed on the table beside him. He was too busy watching the action.

Carolyn and Amanda were back in the living room. They sat together on the sofa, both naked, their legs entwined. Amanda turned to Carolyn and kissed her full on the lips. Pulling apart they both looked up at the webcam and smiled seductively.

"Well, I hope you all enjoyed tonights show, you naughty boys!" said Carolyn teasingly. "We certainly did, didn't we Amanda?"

"Mmm, we sure did. Now don't forget to keep your subscription up to date boys, so you don't miss any of the action!"

"And don't forget to watch us next Monday, seven o'clock sharp."

"Be there or be square!"

Bettina writes,

I've promoted a few things in my time. As a model you are always promoting something or other. You get to meet a lot of new people and if you are lucky travel to exciting places. The girl in this story knows how to take the scenic route, and watch out for that excellent three point turn she performs later on . . .

Promo-girls

PROMO GIRLS

As we shook hands for the first time I realised that for both of us this was to be a great improvement. Kim had said she'd been doing 'in-store promotions' which I know from experience can be deadly boring. My previous summer had been spent on the exhibition circuit handing out endless keyrings and free samples. In our business, girls come and go at a fair rate, but if you persevere and have a good attitude you can end up, like Kim and I, on a cushy, fun-packed and fairly glamourous assignment.

The motorsport calendar runs from April to October, and racing at all levels is heavily sponsored. Kim and I work for a leading drinks company who have a good market-share which includes some wines and spirits. Many of our potential customers are over 18 and therefore our 'company promotions' need a distinctly adult profile. You know, lots of tits and bums, tops that barely cover your boobs, and tiny tight, tight shorts that hardly cover your bum and cut right into your pussy. For promo-girls the summer racing circuit is the best possible posting. Events may be televised and paying spectators can run to several thousands. Perks include hotel accommodation, the freedom to tour Britain, excellent money and of course, a chance to shake your booty for the public and press.

The start grid on race day is also a real buzz. Anyone who shouldn't be there gets turfed out, and for once us promo-girls are in our element.

With the first race of the season drawing near, having Kim for a partner was the icing on the cake. She was tall, had lots of shiny brown hair, a great figure, big tits and a cute arse, and an obvious sense of fun. There was something about her. She had this sort of husky accent which I couldn't quite place.

Our hotel confirmed, we were each handed a 'corporate clothing kit'. This basically consists of a series of uniforms, jackets, sweatshirts, shorts, crop tops, baseball caps, and an umbrella. Kim was also entrusted with the keys to the hire car, and after a short induction session, we were speeding along in search of the Garden Park Hotel, our base for the next few days.

On finding the hotel, Kim dropped me off out front and went away to park. I checked us in and went up to the room. We had twin beds, a TV, an on-suite bathroom and a tall window overlooking the golf-course. I set about trying on some of my clothing kit. I unwrapped the woollen jogging bottoms and a t-shirt with logos on the pockets. Both fitted fine, and to get comfy I walked around in them. I was also dying to try on the shorts that we'd wear on race day, so I stepped out of the trousers to change again. As I stood there in just knickers, t-shirt and trainers Kim walked in.

Now I must admit that as soon as I'd seen Kim at the induction ceremony I'd admired her to a point bordering on sexual. I'd thought to myself that she was attractive and had tried to picture her topless! As she closed the door I decided to follow up this line of enquiry. I had already decided that on this trip I was going to be a bit more sexually adventurous, the trouble was that I had no idea how. The best I could come up with was to linger as long as possible in just these scanty knickers to see what effect it might have. Kim threw all her belongings on the nearest bed and started up a conversation. We just chatted for ages about completely mundane things. I pointed out that there was a golf links under our window and Kim came over to take a look for herself. Beneath us, on a small mound, two golfers caught her eye. Suddenly, she flung back the curtain, turned to me and childishly said, "Hey boys look up here! My friend's flashing her knickers, wanna see some pussy?"

I quickly turned and ran to the far side of the room. Kim just laughed, but her gaze had dropped and she was now checking out my legs. Now I'm a size ten, and I'm particularly proud of my cute, peachy bottom, so as I walked I gave it a seductive wiggle and I think I must have looked quite sexy. Once more and now even more loudly Kim blurted out, "Why don't you show your tits while you're at it?"

Suddenly, I was quite literally in a bit of a corner. I had originally gone across to get away from the window. Now I had to decide whether I was serious about my attempt at seduction. I decided I was. I lifted the t-shirt over my head and the neckline snagged on one of my earrings.

So much for trying to be sexy. I was busy trying to free it without pulling my ear off when I felt a hand on one of my breasts just above my bra line. As an instinctive reaction I almost pulled back but something clicked inside, this is what I wanted.

I stood naively there in matching bra and knickers with the obviously more experienced Kim bearing down on me. I did wonder if she knew that for me this was all fairly new and unexpected, and I was pretty nervous. She became very passionate very quickly and I felt her hot breath against my neck. Almost immediately she began feeling for my strap and expertly unclasped it. Her smooth fingers felt lovely as she massaged my little tits and tweaked my swollen nipples.

"Hang on," she whispered suddenly and went over to close the curtains. She locked the door. "Let's have some fun!" she declared. I wasn't about to argue, and I found the confidence to take a lead. I sat down on the bed, slid backwards and brought my legs up. The soles of my trainers gripped the bedspread and my knees fell open. My pussy was covered by only a thin strip of fabric. Kim stared between my legs as she came back from the door. She knelt of the floor in front of me. She started to gently kiss my legs and lick gradually nearer and nearer to my panties. Her finger traced my pussy through the cotton and eased the fabric to one side to press her tongue against my sex lips.

"Mmm, it's so wet!" Kim purred, "you really are a horny bitch," she said softly as she continued to playfully lick me out. After a few minutes she stopped. She undid her top and leaned forward releasing her firm breasts. They looked soft and had large dark nipples which she pinched to make them really stiff and erect. She pressed them against my pussy and found my clit. She teased me with her nipple and her tit became sticky with my juices, then she squeezed her tit and pointed it upwards to her own mouth to lick my juice from her nipple.

"Now, what can I use to work that pussy with?" she asked, looking around. I felt kind of glad that all the surfaces were bare! But just then she went over to her bag and started rummaging. I looked on, gently rolling my clit with my index finger. She pulled open a company 'snack-pack' and out came a bottle of soft drink. She went into the bathroom and I heard the bottle's contents fizzing down the sink. Coming back to me Kim leaned forwards and began like an artist working on something intricate. With her finger and thumb she opened my pussy and giving the bottle a slow twist she gently inserted it into my tight hole.

"I wonder what a rep from the soft drinks company would say!" said Kim smiling. The bottle's shape was perfect with it's narrow neck and sort of spiralling ribs going down it. I just lay back as she massaged the bottle in and out, and the ribs rubbed against the inside of my cunt and she twisted it home at the end of each stroke. It was heaven. I felt the rush of an orgasm and grabbed at her hair, her thrusting of the bottle got more urgent and rapid and my cum smeared itself down the bottle and over

Kim's wrist and arm.

"Wow you needed that!" exclaimed Kim, licking the rim of the bottle top.

The next day we had to go down to the track and familiarise ourselves with the hospitality suites, changing facilities and general layout. Kim had been down in the morning, and said it was really cool, she couldn't believe how wide the start straight was. I think she expected a normal road with white lines down the middle! I reached the track late in the afternoon, and Kim was right, it was impressive. After showing my pass I managed to wander into the pits area. A good-looking guy came over to greet me. He was late middle-aged and dressed in the garb of a rival team. He introduced himself as Roy, and he asked me if I was enjoying myself and if I had met anyone famous yet. I said I hadn't and we joked around about who it might be good to bump into. I was just trying to figure out what his role was, when he invited me to stop by his workshop later, saying it was the only one unlocked, and where anything interesting was happening.

First I took a walk, and beneath the spectacular grandstand managed to find our sponsorship suite. Sometime later, with an evening chill in the air, I crossed the tarmac to check out the workshops.

Ahead of me was a row of large metal doors, all shut and bolted bar one. I figured it was here that Roy must have meant. I peeped inside and looked around for him.

"Hi! Come on in," he called out in a friendly voice.

Just as earlier, Roy was really charming, he introduced me to two other mechanics, Terry and Paul, who were also there working. I wasn't very interested in what they were doing but quickly noticed how muscled, well-toned and handsome the two younger guys were. They both had blonde hair and were so alike I took them to be brothers. I was then given a tour of the workshop and was shown their team car hidden beneath the dust cover. This led me to ask what they were all doing there so late anyway. There was a bit of laughter and Roy explained that they had been issued with these new kind of walkie talkie headsets and had been sent down to try them out. Terry began speaking into his mike, and joked around pretending to be a pilot asking for permission to land. At this point Roy suggested that they put a headset on me, send me out to walk around and see if they could pick up my signal. It sounded like fun so I said okay.

So there we all were in this spacious, well-lit garage. I'm wearing my team shorts, so small and tight and cut so high my butt cheeks are clearly visible, and my crop t-shirt, cut off so high you can just make out the under side of my boobs. I'm surrounded by Roy and two dreamboat mechanics, both sexy in a silent sort of way, and I'm about to be fitted with this headset. Now what I didn't realise was that there was also a battery pack which had to be worn on a waistband behind my back. I was told to raise my arms and someone passed the belt underneath them. As he did so I felt him accidently - on purpose - brush one of my tits with the back of his hand. Then, Roy and Paul got into difficulties connecting the thing, or at least they pretended to.

"Are you having technical problems?" I asked innocently.

"Just a slight hitch with the wires," replied Roy, sounding flustered.

Next I felt a firm hand between my shoulder blades and a voice simply said, "Get forward and hold still." A second hand pulled at my shorts and I felt a cold strip of wire touch my bum on the inside of my knickers. Low and behold, a hand followed to retrieve it, and seemed to linger. I have to admit to being a wee bit scared but also very excited.

"All correct and ready to go," said Roy.

I felt a bit disappointed and let down. They switched the headset on and my earphones crackled into life. I could clearly hear Roy blowing into his mouthpiece.

"Okay sweetheart, go outside and walk about a bit, tell us what you can hear."

I stepped outside, and with a brilliant reception wherever I went, I began answering Roy through my mouthpiece.

"Yes, I can hear you fine," I said.

"Where are you now, what can you see?"

"Well I can see the other workshops and mostly it's dark, but there's a path straight ahead, and I can see two people walking. They're about a hundred yards ahead, at twelve o'clock! Am I getting the tech-speak right Roy?"

"Yes, you're doing fine. What are they doing then?"

"Well they're holding hands. They've stopped . . . they're kissing."

"Oh, tell me more then!"

"Well, he's put his hand on her bum and oh, he's lifting her skirt now. Wait I'll get in closer . . ."

I caught up with them slightly and I could just make out their faces.

"Are you still there Roy, are you still receiving me . . over?"

"Yes darlin' carry on."

"Now he's pushed her up against a garage door. Her skirt's hitched up around her waist. His hand is inside her panties and they're kissing deeply . . . oh!"

"What is it, what's happening now?" Roy blurted in my ear. I could hear that Roy was getting turned on and I was really enjoying turning him on.

"Now she's undoing his trousers and they've dropped to his ankles. He's got no underwear on. He's got a really cute arse and an enormous erection. He's pulling her panties down. She's wrapping her leg around him with his hand pressing her thigh upwards. She's holding his cock and it looks like . . . yes, she's guiding it into her pussy."

Watching the scene before me, and reporting it back to Roy, was making my pussy really hot. I really envied the woman, having this gorgeous guy fuck her.

"Can you hear the garage door banging Roy, every time he thrusts into her?"

"Yes I can hear that, he's getting quicker isn't he?"

"Yeah, I think he's going to come any moment . . ."

I thought I'd tease Roy by pretending I could hear what the couple were saying.

"Roy, I can just about hear what they are saying. Most of it's moaning and grunting but . . ."

"What are they saying?" Roy asked urgently.

". . . fuck me baby . . . harder . . . yeah - it's so good! . . . ooh . . . you're so deep . . oh yes! Are you getting this Roy?"

"Yeah yeah, carry on."

". . . oh I think I'm coming . . . now, now, yes, yes, now, harder!"

Just as I said this the couple reached their climax, the guy banging into the girl as fast and hard as he could. She screamed with delight. They tidied themselves up and walked on. All that was left was her panties on the floor. I ran to pick them up, and tucked them in my belt. I was going to give them to Roy for a thrill. I hurried back to the workshop, all the while thinking about what could happen if I let it. I remembered the fun I'd had with Kim yesterday, her predatory attitude to life and sex, and this reassured me - these three guys were no problem.

I headed back to the big metal doors and slipped through the gap. Paul and Terry were busy getting on with things trying to look all innocent. Roy was not so reticent, his friendly blue eyes sparkled as he lifted my headset and placed it carefully on the bench.

"Okay princess," he said, "now let's have the battery pack. You're going to have to lean forward again."

I turned round and saw the other two homing in, like

sharks that had smelt the kill. To be honest, I was gagging for it, my pussy was burning hot.

I bent over the bench as far as I could.

"Are you okay with all this?" Roy asked.

We both knew what he meant, that what was about to happen was fairly serious stuff. I nodded and smiled.

"Terry, shut the doors across," commanded Roy.

As Terry sprinted over to the door, my shorts were yanked down, almost pulling me off balance. I felt myself being squeezed and gripped all over. Terry returned, his hands cold from the door, and joined in. One of the guys pulled my little knickers to one side, and I felt his fingers touch my pussy. Someone was eagerly pulling open the cheeks of my bum, and someone else gripped me just above the knee. My legs were positioned so I was standing in a stride, and a finger gently began to rub my arsehole. Then, my knickers were whipped down and I heard someone mutter something. The randy bastards were stroking, groping and finger-fucking me for all they were worth. I stayed down moaning lightly and grinding my arse against their hands.

The next sound I heard was music to my ears. It was the distinctive click of the poppers on the front of their overalls being slowly undone. I rose up and looked round. The guys had backed off and sure enough they were stepping out of their suits. All three were bare chested and walked towards me. Once more my pussy quickly became the centre of attention, Paul and Terry took turns fingering it. Roy was feeling my tits through my t-shirt and kissing me passionately. The intimacy was always a reassuring factor with Roy, and looking back I can remember that every once in a while he had asked me if I was sure I wanted to carry on. Someone caught hold of my arm and I was gently pulled back to the bench. I could see Paul masturbating, he stared straight into my eyes. Roy once more bent me over and I braced myself by holding on to a vice that was bolted to the worktop. Again my bottom was roughly handled and I could feel the tip of Terry's cock nudging at my pussy. I was soaking wet and more than ready to accept what was being offered. Terry massaged his big dick up and down my entire pussy coming dangerously close to my arsehole at the top of each stroke. I could feel the hard head as it agitated my fleshy red lips.

"Roy, hold her still," he said aggressively. The first inch or two was then loaded in and he just stood there, burning a hole in me. Suddenly, and without warning, I felt the bang of a strong pair of male hips against my bottom and I let out a slow, deep moan. His gorgeous cock was now fully inside me, and Terry began pounding. The bench started to creak and I could feel his heavy balls slapping at my entrance. I hadn't been fucked this wantonly for a long time.

Roy, still had his briefs on, he'd been busy holding my shoulders, anchoring me firmly and encouraging his mates. Arching my back I had to slightly redirect Terry's cock inside me, I was literally being nailed to the bench. Paul, meanwhile had come round the front and stuck his stiff dick in my face. I took my cue and letting go of the vice for a second, grabbed it and pulled it towards my mouth. I felt so greedy for cock, it was as if there was nothing else in the world. I let my lips slip up and down its shaft and sucked on it hard and slow.

Roy finally dropped his pants revealing a long, curved dick. He had waited patiently so I let Paul's cock fall from my lips and switched my attention to him. His penis smelt and tasted lovely, all musky, salty and hot. I wanted to give it an especially good blow job, but being fucked so roughly from behind made it difficult. Roy gently held my head with his fingers through my hair. My left hand still clutched at Paul for support more than anything, using his cock like a safety strap on a train. Terry, behind me refused to quit and with increased vigour he stuffed me, banging his cock into me. Next he took it on himself that I needed some extra punishment, and in between strokes, he began bringing his hand down on to my innocent bottom. The combination of all the action and a spanked bum, which I adore, was simply too much to bear, and I felt myself beginning to climax. I had to take a breather from the sucking, and I gasped for air.

"I'm coming, don't stop . . . that's it . . . yes!" I cried out. This only served to encourage them and Roy held me tighter while I was spanked and fucked for dear life. Just as I reached my climax Terry grunted loudly and I felt his hot cum shoot inside me. Then his thrusting became slower, and after a few jerks he pulled out. Now I could concentrate on Roy. I wrapped my lips around his cock and jerked his shaft with my hand. Paul was jerking off, suddenly his thick creamy cum was splashing onto my face and into my hair. Then Roy let out a moan and his cum hit the back of my throat, his cock pulsing in my mouth spurting out hot jets of white sticky salty fluid. I swallowed all of it.

Paul and Terry quickly dressed and were playing with some machinery in one corner, obviously too embarrassed to talk to me.

"Maybe we'll see you at the race track tomorrow?" Roy said.

"I'll look out for you," I said smiling, "I'll be with my friend Kim."

"Perhaps we could all meet up for a drink afterwards. Is she as gorgeous as you?"

"Yeah and she's just as racy!"

I left and looked forward to race day.

Bettina writes,

The title of this story reminds me of when I was at Uni and there were these three girls. They called themselves the x club. They said I could join if I did a little test. I had to give the pizza delivery guy a blow job, no matter what shape or size he came in. Well, I ordered a large vegetarian and ended up with a mouthful of meat. I told him his delivery was wrong, that it was thin and I wanted it deep. I don't often eat an Italian before lunch, but it filled a hole I suppose.

The following story is about a club I would definitely like to join . . .

Joining the club

JOINING THE CLUB

During the drive the feel of her tight cotton panties cutting into her pussy, and her bare inner thighs rubbing against each other produced a series of tiny electric shocks of sexual excitement. She was once again wet between her legs. She was also now in a state of extreme nervous tension, not knowing just what was in store for her at the Club.

She wore a thin, tight, white t-shirt with no bra, a short flimsy black cotton skirt, under which she wore tiny white knickers. On her feet she wore high heels. She'd decided against anything corny like fishnet stockings or a basque, as these struck her as a little too obvious. She didn't want to arrive with soaking wet knickers, so she pulled off the road. Lifting her feet to rest them on the dashboard she eased up her skirt and wriggled out of her panties. She reached into the glove compartment for the spare pair she always kept there in case of emergencies. She was just about to put them on, but decided to wait until she was nearly there as she was so excited they would be wet within minutes.

Gemma was a very sexy, attractive woman, curvy with big baby blue eyes, thick, shoulder length auburn hair and a nubile young body. She'd not been short of offers from men, but hadn't found any of them attractive and didn't really want to get into a relationship since breaking up with her long-term partner Tom. They'd finally split up after the best part of two years spent arguing and being unpleasant to each other. That, together with the fact that she had walked in on him fucking one of her best friends in *her* bed, was the last straw.

Now, at twenty-four, Gemma had been single for almost a year and, in that time, she'd had no sexual experiences with anyone other than herself, but she found she still had no wish to form a relationship with anyone. And in the absence of a real partner, Gemma had created a wild and wonderful fantasy-world of sexual ecstacy, which she hugged to herself every night in bed.

But after a lonely birthday spent sipping wine on her own, she came to the realisation that her fantasies, without some real live sex to give them substance, were becoming more and more difficult to sustain. Gemma knew that today this was all going to change.

She took a second look at the instructions and set off once again for the Club. Driving along she recalled the conversation she'd had with her friend Hayley after bumping into her at Victoria train station.

Over coffee Gemma had begun to tell Hayley some of her recent problems and it was at that point that Hayley first mentioned the Club.

"It's called the Fantasy Club," Hayley had said with a laugh. "It's for people who want to live out their wildest sexual fantasies with like-minded people, but without the bother of any commitment to them afterwards."

"Sounds terrific," said Gemma, "how do you become a member?"

"Oh you just ring this number and say who gave it to you," replied Hayley.

"But who belongs?" Gemma had asked. "I mean supposing I've got a fantasy to have wild sex with a hunky man of thirty and all that's on offer are old men in dirty raincoats."

"No, no!" said Hayley, "it doesn't work like that. Everyone's vetted and, in any case, if you give the name of an existing or past member they'll know it's okay. No one ever recommends anyone they wouldn't want to screw themselves."

"And they've got *sexy* men there?" Gemma had asked, still not convinced.

"And women," smiled Hayley.

A few weeks had passed since Gemma had put the number in her handbag and tried to forget about it.

Then, one day when she was feeling really horny, she took the piece of paper out of her bag and dialled the number before she could change her mind. The phone rang several times and Gemma was just thinking of replacing the receiver when it was answered.

"Hello, my name is Nina, can I help you?" said a soft, sexy voice.

"Er . . . hello," said Gemma nervously. "I was given your number by my friend Hayley Johnson . . ."

Membership of the club was dependent on an initiation. All she'd gleaned from her phone calls with Nina was that she should wear something she felt comfortable and sexy in, and that she was to come along open-minded and prepared for anything.

And now, initiation day had come and she was minutes away from the Club. Shivers of anticipation ran through her body as she pushed her foot down hard on the accelerator.

Eventually she found herself coasting up a long drive to a very stately house. She stopped the car, slipped on her fresh pair of panties and stepped out on to a hard gravel drive. On unsteady legs, she made her way to the vast wooden front door. She rang the bell, then hurriedly put on a pair of sun-glasses to give an impression of coolness that she certainly didn't feel.

The door was opened by a pretty young girl wearing a maids uniform, just about. Her full young breasts were barely contained within the tight low cut neckline of the black dress, and Gemma guessed she wouldn't have to bend very far forward at all for the little flared dress to spring up revealing her cute bottom.

"Gemma?" asked the girl, giving a delicious dimpled smile.

"Yes," Gemma said, taking off her sunglasses.

"Please come in. I'm Nina. You're exactly how I had imagined you."

Gemma was taken into a large wood-panelled hallway and told to sit in a huge old armchair. Nina disappeared for a while, then returned with some instructions. Nina was to blindfold Gemma and then take her to the initiation room.

With her stomach beginning to somersault in anxious anticipation, Gemma stood still while Nina stepped round behind her with the blindfold. She put the strip of black velvet across Gemma's eyes and tied it at the back. As she did so, Gemma felt Nina's breasts pushing into her back. The blindfold was tied as tightly as possible and then Nina rested her hands lightly on Gemma's shoulders for a second. Then she gently turned her round several times so Gemma lost all sense of direction. Finally she was brought to a halt, and Nina came up so close to her that Gemma could feel the young girl's hot breath on her face, and for a second she wondered if Nina was going to kiss her.

Dry-mouthed with tension, Gemma felt her hand being gently taken by her new companion. A sharp intake of breath must have betrayed her anxiety, for Nina whispered in her ear.

"Don't be afraid, Gemma. I promise you'll come to no harm. The club promotes only pleasure, and that's what you'll have, believe me."

Scarcely reassured, Gemma responded to Nina's prompting and allowed herself to be led slowly down the long corridor ahead of her.

As she heard the sound of her own high heels clacking along the polished wooden floor and her short skirt swishing against her bare thighs, it was all she could do to resist the urge to tear the blindfold from her eyes and run wildly out of the building. In her heart she began to wish she'd never heard of the Club, never made that fateful phone call, never agreed to Nina's softly spoken blandishments to 'come along and just see how she got on'. And yet . . . and yet, between her legs she was aware of a burning desire.

After walking for some time, they finally came to a doorway, and stepping through they came to a halt. As the door shut behind the pair, Gemma seemed to smell the mustiness of old books, but felt also that it was quite a large room. Clearly there were other people present, but who they were and of what sex, Gemma had no idea. Butterflies restarted in her stomach and again she had to resist the urge to flee.

"This is Gemma," announced Nina whilst still holding onto Gemma's hand.

"Excellent! Stunning!" said a woman's voice and a hot shock-wave flooded through Gemma's body.

"You can stay or leave Nina, it's up to you," the woman continued.

Gemma squeezed Nina's hand in terror at the thought of being left, and Nina gave her an answering squeeze.

"I'll stay Miss," she said.

"I don't blame you," said the woman, with what was probably a smile. "Now Gemma, move into the centre of the room."

Nina propelled Gemma forward and she took three or

four steps on the hard wood floor until the woman commanded her to stop. She was then told to turn round slowly, and did so, aware that any number of eyes could be mentally undressing her, and she had no idea of how many, or to whom they belonged. Eventually the woman's voice bid her stop and she did so.

There followed a long silence. She stood for a while until she became aware that another person, or persons, had moved to stand in front of her. The heat of a body was just distinguishable and she stiffened slightly in anticipation. And then, suddenly, a hand touched her gently on the cheek and Gemma started with surprise. The hand stroked her cheek and was joined by another on the other cheek. The hands felt soft and Gemma wondered whether they were Nina's or another woman's. They felt too soft for a man's. But, before she had time to think anymore, her face was pulled forward by the hands and lips were lightly brushing her face, tracing patterns across the skin, and taking tiny bites at it. The lips circled round and slowly came to rest on Gemma's neck. The exquisitely warm lips opened wider and a tongue forced it's way between Gemma's lips and delicately licked her teeth.

Gemma resisted at first. The softness of the lips, hands and face told her this was a woman she was kissing. She wasn't convinced it was something she wanted, but the lips were warm, and she began to respond in kind. The two tongues started to link and twist together. Her hands automatically moved towards the face of the person kissing her so purposefully, but to her surprise they were grabbed by other hands from behind her and held there. She continued to kiss the unseen lips but accepted that she wasn't to touch and, when the person behind her released her hands she obediently left them by her side.

The two hands at the back now slid onto the waistband of her skirt, felt along to the zip undid it and slowly slipped the skirt down Gemma's long bare legs. She gasped slightly as the unseen hands made there way back up her legs and onto her upper thighs, and she found herself slightly widening her legs to allow the hands access to her more intimate parts. The hands stayed just below her buttocks, caressing the flesh of her upper thighs, and two thumbs gently inched in towards her pussy. Again they felt too soft for a man's hands and Gemma was convinced the flames of her desire were being fired by two women.

In the meantime she was still firmly kissing and being kissed by the other person. Soon she felt the hands move from her face down to her shoulders, and then down her sides and then onto her waist. They took hold of the t-shirt edge and slowly lifted it up and over Gemma's head, breaking off the kiss for a second, so that the whole of her upper body was now completely naked. The hands disposed of the t-shirt and swiftly returned to Gemma's neck to bring her head forward for a resumption of the kiss. They then began to caress her. First her shoulders, then her arms, and finally circling round to her firm upright breasts. The hands cupped each breast gently and then began to stroke and lightly flick the nipples until they became so stiff they almost ached. And then the lips left hers, worked their way down Gemma's neck to her breasts and began to suck and nibble, first one nipple then the other.

Gemma felt her pussy getting even wetter and she thrust her body forward to reach that of the owner of those tantalizing and exciting lips. But she could make no contact and suddenly felt her little cotton pants being sharply tugged off by the hands at her back. They were pulled down her legs to the floor where she stepped out of them. She was now naked except for high-heels. Hands firmly pushed her forward so she was bending right over, as if about to be caned, and those same hands then slid over her back and down across the tightly stretched skin of her bottom. They came up under her and lightly caressed the inside of her thighs, all the while nudging them apart. Fingers fluttered around the lips of her vagina, and she felt the first tremors of an orgasm starting deep within her body.

Then suddenly Smack! Smack! Smack! She felt three sharp slaps to her bare behind. But, even as the stinging sensation was making itself felt, the fingers were now inserting themselves right into the moistness of her pussy, and gently stroking her clitoris which felt larger and more tender than ever before. And still those soft lips and hands sucked and stroked at her swollen breasts.

Then came three more sharp smacks to her arse, ringing out around the room and stinging more this time.

"Oh!" cried Gemma, in a mixture of ecstasy and pain. As the hands slid back down the deep and inviting cleft of her bottom to lightly tickle the rim of her anus, she suddenly found herself shuddering to a climax.

But even as she surrendered to the first onrush of sweet pleasure, hands took her head and pulled it forward to meet a thick hard cock which slipped into her mouth, between the parted lips of ecstasy.

Shocked that there was, after all, at least one man present, Gemma nevertheless quickly began to mouth the cock with gentle sucking motions, and could not resist putting out her hands to pull the man closer to her. She encountered muscled thighs and allowed her hands to slide round and firmly grasp the tight buttocks of the man whose cock she could now feel coming to a climax of its own. She dug her nails into the firm flesh of the male cheeks and felt, rather than heard the man shudder with explicit pleasure. As her fingers slid into the cleft between his buttocks his actions became more jerky and uncontrolled and suddenly he came inside her mouth. Hot jets hitting the back of her throat.

With her own next climax beginning to swell again, she swallowed the salty sticky fluid. However, as she allowed her mouth to relax around the still swollen penis, she realised that another was entering her from behind. The cock, which now slid into her soaking wet pussy, felt bigger than any she'd ever seen or heard of, and she gasped as the man to whom it belonged thrust against her still smarting buttocks, pushing himself right up inside her.

At first she thought it was too large and wanted to cry out as the great thick organ seemed to stretch the walls of her vagina to snapping point. But then she knew she could take it without pain, and waves of pleasure began to flood through her body. Again and again he slid his enormous penis in and out, causing Gemma to reach new and unexpected heights of excitement, as she bucked and thrust her hips back onto him. Hands were all over her body but she no longer knew how many people were taking their pleasure from her. Naked flesh rubbed against her from all sides, and she was vaguely aware of little thrills in parts of her she'd never thought of as erogenous, and much sharper thrills and sparks of electricity all over her naked body. But mostly she knew only the thrusting of the penis sliding into her as far as it could go and then slowly out, then in again and out. As the powerful thrust increased in tempo, Gemma began to come in great rippling waves, crying out in abandoned, exhausted ecstasy as the cock seemed to dig deeper and deeper inside her. And then the man came with furious spurts far into her body as they screamed out their pleasure together and a vast shuddering orgasm overtook both of them.

And then it was over.

Eventually the man withdrew, and the others left Gemma's immediate vicinity. She was led by the hand to a sofa on which she lay back, overwhelmed with physical and emotional tiredness, but feeling more fulfilled than she could ever remember. And then the woman's voice rang out.

"Well done Gemma, you are now a member of our Club - welcome."

Gemma felt happy that she had pleased, and wanted to see for herself who had pleasured her so thoroughly and expertly. Especially she wanted to see the owner of that enormous cock, to see if he was as wonderful to look at as he had been to feel inside her. But then she felt the blindfold being removed and she was in a room with only Nina for company, a Nina it might be said who was also as naked as Gemma herself. Gemma took in her pleasingly plump little body, and was glad to think Nina had been one of those giving her such enjoyment, but nevertheless she looked quickly around to see who else might still be there. Her disappointment must have shown.

"Don't worry," said Nina with a smile, "you'll meet all of them again. And others."

"Especially him," said Gemma, "the big one?"

"Yes, I thought you were particularly enjoying him," said Nina. "Now come along with me, I'm going to help you relax by giving you a nice hot bath."

"Mm," smiled Gemma, "sounds nice. Though you might have to be gentle with me at first."

Nina grinned, took Gemma's hand and the two women headed off for the bathroom and another date with pleasure. Gemma decided she was going to like this Club.

Bettina writes,

If you've read the first story in this book then you may want to know how Katrina got on when she returned to Adrian's studio.

I arranged a second photo shoot with her. During the shoot I probed her for more information about her naughty introduction to the world of modelling.

As she told me all about it I tried to stay focused, but her dirty talk got me hot for some of that girly action. She used all the right words in all the right places. I made sure she told me everything so I could relate it to you. Katrina and her friends really know how to play up for the camera . . .

So load up boys and get ready to shoot . . .

I couldn't help it, Episode 2:
Katrina and Nikki

KATRINA AND NIKKI

After making the solo video I was buzzing. I was too excited to go back to my lonely bedsit, so I went to see my college friend, Ann. She shares a house with another girl, Nita and three boys.

Nita answered the door. I noticed she'd had her hair cut short, slightly boyish I thought. She looked cute, it really suited her.

"Hi Nita, is Ann around?" I asked.

"No Katrina you've just missed her, she's gone out with Adam and Tony. Come in though, it's nice to see you. I've just finished revising, I could do with a good natter."

I followed Nita up to her room. It wasn't very big, just enough space for a bed and a small table. The only redeeming point was it had a nice view overlooking the garden.

"Tea or coffee?"

"I'll have tea, thanks."

Nita flicked the switch on the electric kettle and then knelt on the floor, her head and shoulders disappearing under the bed.

"Where is it? I know I've got another mug under here somewhere."

As Nita searched for the coffee mug, her short skirt did nothing to hide her cute lilac panties, which had inched their way up into the crack of her bottom.

Since making the video I felt so much more sexually aware. I began to look at Nita as a sex object, although I had met her on numerous occasions and it had never crossed my mind before.

The thin cotton was stretched tight across Nita's cute bum. I felt like reaching out, I wondered how she would react. Her skin was smooth and a lovely light brown in colour.

"I've found it!" Nita exclaimed, reappearing holding a plastic container. Peeling the lid off she produced a 'Starsky and Hutch' mug. "I keep this in case I have guests, which as you probably figured isn't very often. Tea wasn't it?"

"Yes please, two sugars. I really like your hair Nita. It suits you like that."

"Oh thanks, I only got it done last week. That new place in the high street, it does discounts for students."

"I'll have to go there. Do you think it would suit me short too?"

"It probably would suit you but I really like it the way it is."

Nita handed me my tea. "Have a biscuit, there's a packet of custard creams on the window sill."

I leaned across the bed and helped myself, putting some of the biscuits on a plate.

"Well, what have you been up to today?" asked Nita.

"You'll never guess," I said rather smugly.

"Well let me see . . ." Nita grinned, "you went to see a man about a sleazy film. Am I right?"

"You knew! Ann must have told you."

"Yeah, when she got in from college it was all she could talk about. Well spill it, what happened?"

"I did it!" I blurted out. "I made a movie."

"You didn't!"

"I did!" I opened my bag and pulled out the three hundred pounds and threw it on the bed.

"Wow, you got paid that much. What did you have to do?"

"Well, promise you won't tell any of the boys, otherwise I'll never hear the last of it."

"I promise, now tell me *exactly* what happened - right from the beginning."

"I was just gonna go there and see what went on, you know, just have a look around. Well, when I got there he was just about to start filming a girl called Nikki, she was dressed up as a nurse, in one of those sexy Ann Summers outfits."

"Hang on, who was about to start filming?"

"Oh yeah, Adrian, he's the guy who owns the studio. He's thirty-something, not bad looking either for his age. He told me he sells the films on the internet, and that they sell well too. That's how he can afford to pay this much. Anyway, Adrian said I could watch Nikki do her set, so I'd know what I'd be letting myself in for." I took a sip of tea.

"What did she do?"

"Well, she stripped off her uniform, pretending that the camera was a patient, you know, like she was putting on a show for a patient. Then she started to play with herself."

"No!"

"Yeah, she played with herself . . . till she came."

"Wow! I know we all do it, but I don't think I could do it in front of someone."

"I did." I whispered, almost apologetically.

There was silence. We both sipped our tea, and both took a biscuit off the plate. Nita just looked at me with a custard cream poised between her lips.

"You didn't!"

"I did." I replied, this time with a bit more conviction.

"I can't believe you did that!"

"I was a bit nervous at first, but it was okay once I got started, and then I really got into it."

"And you came and everything?" asked Nita nearly choking on a mouthful of custard cream.

"Yeah, I found it a real buzz to do it in front of the camera - there's nothing wrong with it you know - I'm looking forward to doing it again."

"You're doing it again?"

"Yes, next week, with the girl I watched, Nikki. She's really nice. She suggested we could do a shoot together. You know, a girl/girl thing."

"So are you going to kiss her, and touch her, and everything?" asked Nita, wide-eyed with surprise.

"Yeah. It's not like I've done it before, but I think I can do it. She's very cute you know. Anyway she said she'd help me."

Nita put her tea down. "Even so, if you've never done it before it'll be kind of weird won't it?"

"Well I'm kind of curious anyway, about what it would be like. Haven't you ever wanted to then, you know, do it with a girl?" I asked, moving a bit closer, hoping the answer would be yes.

"Well, when I was about thirteen I practised kissing with my best friend back home, but it was just playing about. We didn't really mean it. But looking back, yeah I did kind of like it."

"Don't you ever look at girls and think, yeah she's sexy?"

"Well, yeah sometimes."

"Don't you ever fantasize about women? I know I do."

"I suppose . . ."

I looked at her, gazing into her eyes.

"Nita . . ." I ventured, "do you mind if I kiss you . . ?" I continued tentatively. "Like you said, I need some practise, don't I, if I'm going to make it look really good in the movie."

Nina looked surprised and before she could answer, I leaned forward to kiss her. First of all we just sort of touched lips, and then when I found no resistance, I got more confident and opened my mouth slightly. Still no resistance, and Nita opened her lips in response. I felt the heat building in my pussy and wanted to slip my hand between her legs, but I didn't know how she would react, and I wasn't going to take the chance of going too far. I drew away and just looked at her for a moment. Her eyes were closed, and her mouth open.

"Wow!"

"Yeah, wow!"

The following Wednesday, I went back to Peckham to see Adrian for another film shoot. I was a bit nervous but I knew Nikki would be there to help me if I found I didn't know what to do. Nita decided she wanted to come along, 'just to watch' she said.

Adrian answered the door.

"Hi Katrina, nice to see you again, who's your friend?" he said looking Nita up and down.

"This is Nita. I hope you don't mind my bringing her, she won't get in the way, she's just come to keep me company."

"No I don't mind, come in, come in. Go straight up to the studio girls. Nikki's already here."

We climbed the stairs and walked into the big room.

"I've set up a little jail scene for you and Nikki," said Adrian pointing to the far corner of the room. I looked over and saw a single bed on the wooden floor and a fake window built behind it.

"Oh, it looks so realistic," I said going over to have a

closer look. "I love the bars at the window."

Nikki popped her head out from behind the screen.

"Hi Katrina! Great to see you", she said smiling. "I'm glad you decided to do a girl/girl with me. Come behind here and I'll show you what Adrian wants us to wear. Who's your friend?"

"This is Nita, I hope you don't mind if she hangs around while we film today."

Nikki smiled again, "No! I don't mind at all . . . she's cute! Has she come to see if she wants a go in front of the camera?"

Adrian laughed and turned to Nita, "Oh she'll be wanting to do a girl/girl with *you* next, sweetheart. She wants *all* the good-looking girls!"

Nita blushed and giggled. I went behind the screen with Nikki to look at the clothes.

"Come and have a look at this, Nita," Adrian gushed. "Are you interested in film-making at all?" He pointed to a TV screen. "I'm editing a short film I made yesterday. I'm cutting out the bits where the girl started to giggle. It's quite tricky getting the action to join smoothly, but I have a lot of experience now. I think it's going to be a really good one when it's done. What do you think sweetheart?"

"Yeah, she's really pretty," said Nita, still blushing bright red. "She's really beautiful. Has she had a boob job?" she added pointing at the TV screen.

"Well I don't know, I didn't get to feel them sweetheart, but they look great anyway don't they?"

"Yeah, they do look good . . . better than mine," said Nita looking down.

Adrian looked closely at her chest. "You've got just as good a figure as she has - ever thought of doing anything like this yourself . . ."

Nikki looked up, "Stop drooling over Nita, Adrian," she said winking at me. "We're ready now, come and look."

"Wow!" he said looking up at us.

Nikki and I had put on our clothes and we did look pretty hot!

"This is gonna be one hell of a sexy video," exclaimed Adrian, getting up from the sofa he'd been sharing with Nita. "The clothes I picked are perfect. Even if I say it myself - I've really got good taste."

I was wearing a very short flowery cotton dress that had buttons all the way down the front, white panties and showgirl shoes. Nikki was wearing the police girls uniform she had admired when I first met her. Shiny black PVC, a zip down the front, a belt around the waist, and knee length black leather boots to kick with. She really looked the part. Thick, glossy red lipstick covered her sensuous mouth.

"I'm going to fuck and lick you senseless," Nikki whispered in my ear as we walked over to the set. Her unexpected words made me tingle all over.

"So, Katrina, you're going to be a girl in trouble with the police. You've been arrested for disgusting behaviour in a public place. Nikki is the police woman who has brought you to the cell. She asks you what you were caught doing. You tell her that you were caught going down on your boyfriend in a shopping mall. I'll let you girls take it from there . . . okay then, are you ready?"

We said yes, and he started to film us.

Nikki grabbed my arm and made like she was pulling me into the cell.

"Now I don't want any trouble from *you*," she said sternly. "You'll be seeing the judge in the morning. What you in here for anyway, shoplifting I suppose. What was it make-up or clothes?"

"Neither actually, I don't have to steal, I have money. Lots of it."

"Well then Miss La di da, what did you do? Don't tell me you're another innocent person the justice system locked up!"

"I didn't commit a crime, I'm not a criminal. I just got a bit carried away that's all. I didn't know anyone was watching, anyway they should mind their own business. If I want to suck my boyfriend off in a shopping mall I will."

"You what? You sucked your boyfriend's dick in a shopping mall! Are you mad?"

"No, I was horny! I couldn't help it. Haven't you ever done anything like that?"

"No way! I prefer pussy."

"You mean you're a dyke? Sorry I mean a lesbian. What pleasure can you get from that, I mean, no offence, but without a dick what can you do?" I sat back on the mattress deliberately letting my dress ride up my thighs a bit. "My boyfriend's dick is so hard, so long, and so thick, there isn't anything like it."

Nikki produced her truncheon from the side pocket of her outfit. It was long and black and about as phallic as it could be without actually having veins down it! She stroked it lightly with her long red fingernails.

"Is it as big as this?" Nikki asked, looking down at me.

I glanced over and saw Nina watching us intently, wide-eyed and flushed. Adrian was walking around us with a hand held camera, and every time he got between us and Nina, she would lean around him to get a better view.

Nikki slipped the truncheon back into its pocket. She reached round to the back of her belt and unclipped a pair of chrome handcuffs. I wriggled around as she tried to clip them on to my wrists, pretending like I was trying to get away.

"Keep still, bitch!" she ordered, pushing me down on to the bed.

I ended up lying face down with my arms handcuffed behind me. Nikki pulled me up into a sitting position, and as I leaned against the metal headboard, she pushed up my dress and pulled down my panties, almost ripping them off me.

"Now you'll find out what girls do . . ."

"No!" I protested, squirming around, "don't touch me you . . ."

"Hey bitch keep quiet, you'll enjoy it, you'll see. You'll never want a man again. "

Nikki knelt on the bed in front of me. I was helpless and I pretended to kick my legs in feigned struggle. She grabbed them and held them down.

"Keep still slut . . . " she said sternly and pushed my legs apart. "Now I'm gonna show you what it's *really* like . . ."

"No! No! Leave me alone! I'm not that kind of girl, please don't . . ."

Nikki leaned forward and put her head between my legs and with one long lick sent shivers through me.

"Ooh pussy - my favourite!" she said looking up into my eyes.

"Leave my pussy alone, don't touch it," I protested again, wriggling and struggling some more. "It's only for my boyfriend."

"Well he's gonna have to share isn't he, he can't have it all for himself."

Nikki spread my pussy lips with her fingertips and ran the tip of her tongue round my clitoris. I was really hot for her and I wanted her to really suck me. She still teased me and I started to gasp a little. She looked up at me and realised the effect she was having.

"So, you're starting to like it huh?"

"No, not at all!" I lied.

Nikki sat up and started unbuttoning the front of my dress exposing my breasts. She pulled the dress down off my shoulders, and licked and sucked my nipples. Then I felt her hand between my legs, she pushed a finger into my cunt.

"Oh, stop, stop . . ." I whispered softly, but really meaning yes, yes.

She ran her tongue up my neck and kissed me on the lips. This time I responded, forcing my tongue inside her mouth. Our kissing was passionate and hot. I broke away. My own feelings took over and I didn't need to act anymore.

"Undo my handcuffs . . . please."

"So you do like it then, bitch."

Nikki reached for the key and unlocked the cuffs. I slipped them from my wrists. Nikki stood up, pulled my dress right off and threw it on the floor. I was naked except for my shoes. I sat on the edge of the bed. Nikki unbuckled her belt, then slowly unzipped the front of her uniform. She stepped towards me. I reached up and ran my hands over her beautiful breasts, her nipples were hard and erect.

Nikki lay on the bed, spread her legs wide and ran a finger over her pussy, pushing the white panty cotton into her hole. "Taste it, bitch!" she ordered, tugging her panties down so I could have access to her neatly shaven cunt.

I knelt on the bed, leaning forward on my elbows, my arse high. I had my legs apart so that Adrian had a good shot of my bum and pussy. I looked up at Nikki, she knew this was my first time.

"Go on then . . ." she said, her beautiful eyes gleaming.

I placed my hands on her tummy and slowly licked her clitoris.

"Oh yeah, that's good," she purred, encouraging me to continue. "Lick it, go on."

I did as she said and she pulled gently at my hair.

It suddenly flashed into my mind that Nina was still watching us just fifteen feet or so away. At that moment though, I didn't care who was watching me. I was feeling so hot and horny. All I could think about was Nikki and giving her pleasure.

"Ooh you're a quick learner. That lovely tongue of yours . . . better than any guy's prick . . . put it inside my cunt . . . "

I spread Nikki's pussy lips and licked the pretty pink flesh. Her pussy was so wet it glistened. "Mmm . . . this is so sweet, so different to sucking off my boyfriend," I said looking up at Nikki for her approval. Then again I pressed my tongue to her pussy, tasting her sweet girly-cum.

Nikki's fingers found her own clitoris, and as I licked and probed she expertly caressed and played with herself. Her breathing deepened and quickened, she spread her legs as wide as she could. With her free hand she held my head, pulling at my hair as I teased her, my eager tongue flicking back and forth, eating her, bringing her to orgasm.

"Yes bitch . . . faster . . . faster . . . I'm going to come, yes, yes!"

Nikki's whole body shook as she climaxed. I slowed

down as her finger left her clit.

"Ooh that was so lovely," she sighed, her fingers stroking my hair. She relaxed, lying back on the bed. "Now I think you deserve a good hard fucking, what do you think?"

"Yes I do," I said, I was so horny, my pussy was so hot for her.

As Nikki reached for the truncheon I felt a thrill of anticipation ripple through me. The truncheon was big and I wasn't sure I could take it however wet I was. But Nikki knew what she was doing I was sure of that. I lay on my back and drew up my legs giving Adrian the best view of my pussy I could.

"So, what is it you want?" teased Nikki.

"A good hard fucking . . . I need a good hard fucking."

"You didn't say *please* . . ."

"*Please* fuck me," I said in my best begging tone.

Nikki picked up the truncheon and licked the end. It felt cold as it brushed against my thigh. She pushed one finger, and then two into my pussy.

"Hey you're ready for this alright - you're *so* wet. You horny bitch, you want it bad don't you? Come on, tell me so."

"I want it bad. Give it to me . . . *please* . . . fuck me hard . . ."

"That's more like it, I knew you wanted me to fuck you all along."

Nikki pushed the tip of the truncheon inside my cunt,

it felt steely cold and hard as ice. She kissed me as she pushed it further inside, I opened my mouth to gasp and she covered it with her lips, pushing her tongue inside as the truncheon went up inside me. I felt the girth of the truncheon squeeze tightly inside me and the motion of it felt good in Nikki's expert hands. She really knew what she was doing, and I wasn't going to be able to hold off from coming for long.

"I'm going to come! I'm going to come - now!" I managed to get the words out and pulled my mouth away from hers to let out a scream as my orgasm ripped through my body.

Nikki and I lay back on the bed, our bodies entwined. She smiled broadly, "Welcome to the wonderful world of pussy, kid - as a great man once said."

Adrian put down the camera. "Brilliant girls! I think I need a cold shower! What did you think of that Nita?"

"Wow!"

A week later on the Thursday morning I was just having breakfast when Nita phoned. She sounded really excited and wanted to come round to see me. When she arrived she was bounding with energy and full of excitement. I made us a coffee and told her to sit still long enough to tell me what she was so excited about.

"I did it!" she announced with a big smile.

"I thought so! The way you sounded on the phone.

And the way you looked at me when I was with Nikki, I thought to myself it won't be long before she's having a go herself. What did you do? When did you go?"

"Well I rang Adrian the day after we went to his studio. He said to come right over if I wanted to. So I did."

"So what did you do then? Tell me." I really wanted *all* the details, I couldn't believe Nita had come out of herself so much so soon. "And why did you decide to do it after all?" I had so many questions.

"Well, it was seeing you, and Nikki. It really turned me on. And Adrian seemed like such an ordinary guy, not seedy you know like you'd imagine. I think he's quite good looking as well. I could quite fancy him. But he never tries it on though does he?"

"No. I asked Nikki what he was like, whether he had ever tried it on with her, and she said no, he never has - and she's been there lots of times. In fact she said she had deliberately tried to turn him on but with no apparent success." I sipped my coffee and let Nita tell me more.

"It's so exciting isn't it, being filmed, doing it for the camera - I never thought I could do something like that. But with Adrian you just can. It's like he's not there, but at the same time you're so aware of yourself, and of what you're doing, and so aware of how good he wants it to look that you give him exactly what he wants."

"Hold on, I'll just get the biscuits." I went to the kitchen, all the time my mind racing with images of Nita writhing in front of the camera. I was getting so horny just thinking about it that I nearly dropped the biscuits all over the floor. I sat back down next to Nita and offered the tin to her. "So, did you actually come, or did you fake it?" I had to know.

"Well I didn't think I could, but I really came. I just relaxed and got into it. It took me a while to warm up, but then it was really good once I had got into the scene, and Adrian said I was brilliant."

"What was the scenario you were playing out?"

"I was a college girl. The idea of the scene was that I was being spied on through my window by a peeping tom. Adrian said it would be an easy scene for me to begin with because I wouldn't have to do any speech or look at the camera. He told me to start off by looking under my room-mates bed, pull out a box of dirty magazines, and act like I was surprised to discover them there. Then I had to take one out and lie on the bed and read it. As I turned the pages he told me to pretend to be shocked, and you know, that wasn't difficult, because I've never even read one in real life! Then as I lay there looking through it I began to get turned on, and started to touch myself a little. And then, *you know*, I did it."

"When I did mine, I enjoyed it so much I really wanted to do it again. Are you going to go back?"

"Well, Adrian wants me to. He even suggested that I do a double with you . . ." Nita trailed off, her face blushing pink. She took another mouthful of coffee.

I saw that she was embarrassed by what she had said, so I quickly blurted out, "Yes, that would be good, I'd love to and since, you know, we have already *kissed* . . ."

Nita's face went even redder. I moved a bit closer to her, and we looked into each others eyes and kissed. Her breath tasted sweet. The gentleness turned to passion and I pushed her down onto my bed.

I was on top of her, our lips pressed together, our mouths open, exploring each other. My hands were all over her, caressing every part of her body through her clothes. Her outfit was tight and close fitting; a short pink mini skirt and a pale yellow fluffy angora sweater that clung to her curves. I suddenly felt a hand between my legs, her fingers were rubbing my pussy through my panties. My skirt was up round my waist and my clitoris was on fire under her fingers.

"Tell me more about what you did for Adrian . . ." I said, breathless, "did you use the vibrator?" My hands squeezed Nita's breasts through her jumper.

"Yes I did," she sighed, slightly short of breath.

As her fingers still teased me, I pulled the low neck of her jumper down below her breasts which were encased in an elaborate pink lacy bra, and fondled her nipples through the lace.

"What did you do with it?"

"I rubbed it against my pussy . . ."

Her fingers played with my clit through the thin cotton fabric of my panties, now becoming wet through. I was so hot and horny for her.

"How did it feel? I panted.

"It was really . . . good . . ." she gasped.

"What like this?" I asked sliding my hand down inside her knickers between her legs. Pressing quite hard, my hand found the entrance to her pussy. I slipped two fingers inside.

"Ooh . . ." Nita writhed beneath me. Our clothed bodies rubbed against each other, the friction between us aroused us even more.

"Then what did you do with it?" I encouraged her to talk dirty to me. It excited me.

"I pushed it inside me . . . imagined it was Adrian's cock sliding in and out . . . and he was really giving it to me . . . I felt like such a slut . . . such a tart, and I was so horny for it . . ."

Nita's pussy was so wet and my fingers slid easily in and out. I pushed them in deeper. She in turn pulled at my panties, sliding her hand inside she massaged my clit, alternately dipping her fingers inside my cunt. I couldn't take much more. Our breathing was getting faster and faster, our fingers quickened.

"Ooh Katrina . . . do it harder, yes . . . yes . . . deeper . . . kiss me . . . fuck me . . ."

I was really getting off on her dirty talk and I kissed her deeply. My tongue in her mouth pushed her over the edge and she came, crying out as my mouth covered hers, writhing under me. Her orgasm prompted mine and I felt my climax rise in me as she finger-fucked me really fast.

We lay entwined on the bed, kissing and caressing each other.

The doorbell rang.

"Oh who is that. Oh, I guess I'd better answer it. I

won't be a minute." I got off the bed and straightened my clothes.

I opened the door. It was Ann.

"Hi Katrina, thought I'd pop in and see how you are. I haven't seen you for a while. How did that video thing go?"

"Come in Ann," I said smiling, "and we'll tell you all about it . . ."

Bettina writes,

I love travelling in Europe, the people are so relaxed and friendly. Now some people go abroad to get a tan, this guy had something else in mind . . .

Just Relax Señor

JUST RELAX SENOR

Tony picked up the phone and dialled the 'Relax' number he'd found in 'El Pais'.

A woman's voice answered "Si?"

"I want a girl for this evening please," said Tony.

"When?"

"As soon as possible."

"How will you pay?"

He paid with his credit card, and gave the woman his personal details, name, hotel, room number, and the deal was clinched. Tony could hardly believe how easy it had been!

"The girl is called Pilar," said the woman. "She is young and very pretty."

Half an hour later came a light tap at the door. Quickly, Tony got up, wondering what she'd be like, this girl he'd booked on the phone. Would she be as pretty as the woman claimed? He doubted it, but as long as she was passable and pleasant and willing to have sex, that was all he was bothered about.

He opened the door. She was a gem; with a face like a dream! Olive complexion, hair and eyes as black as jet, crimson sensual lips. And her figure! Breasts with almost visible nipples thanks to her plunging neckline, a wasp waist you could span with two hands and long slim legs that went on for ever but still managed to show plenty of thigh thanks to her short, short mini skirt.

Tony had an erection on the spot, especially as this ravishing creature was leaning sexily against the door, her lips sensually sucking on one of her fingers.

"Tony?" she said with a cool smile removing her finger from her mouth, he nodded dumbly. "I'm Pilar."

"Come in, please," Tony managed to gasp. "You're very prompt."

"I like to give good value for money," smiled the girl. "What can I do for you?" She sat on the bed and crossed her legs, causing the bulge in Tony's trousers to be more noticeable than ever. Embarrassed he turned away, trying to get himself more comfortable. She just grinned, her hands moving to her lap. She uncrossed her legs and allowed her thighs to part. She wore no panties underneath.

"Shall I masturbate for you?" she whispered.

"Yes please," Tony sighed.

"Just a moment then, *querido*, you'll want to be comfortable, won't you? Just lie on the bed while I fix things up."

Tony lay down obediently, while she opened the wardrobe in front of the bed, revealing a large mirror.

"Nice, eh?" Pilar grinned, joining Tony on the bed. "Now watch. Look into the mirror and you will see something very interesting . . ." She giggled.

They both stared as with a wanton smile Pilar opened her legs as wide as her skirt would allow; which in practice was as far as she wanted, the skirt providing no restriction whatsoever. Tony had a grandstand view of her pretty pussy, surrounded by thick black pubic hair.

"You like?" she smiled, and Tony nodded. "Watch," she said.

She raised her knees and put both hands to her cunt.

"Have you seen a girl masturbate before?" she asked. Tony shook his head breathless, he was very young, very inexperienced, and not in his wildest dreams had he imagined that he would be seeing the scene which now unfolded before him. His cock was rock hard! Pilar ran a painted nail down its length through the material of his trousers.

"Ooh Tony this is a nice big treat for me later," she purred, trailing her finger back up to the top of his throbbing erection.

Pilar laughed and carried on playing with herself, while Tony stared in fascinated wonder at the mirror, his eyes growing ever rounder as she deftly fingered her pink lips. His cock was beginning to ache meantime, but he didn't want to take it out, not yet anyway.

He was happy to watch Pilar's agile fingers, rubbing up and down her cunt till it was soaking wet. Then she teased open her pussy lips and pushed a finger inside caressing her clitoris with her thumb. Pilar began to breathe heavily as the movement excited her. She was starting to writhe and pushed her bottom off the bed so Tony could see her puckered arsehole. Both hands massaged the soft downy skin between her anus and pussy, and he was in agony now.

"Go on, wank, *querido*," gasped Pilar, breathless from her own pleasure.

Tony tore down his zipper and pulled out his hard cock. A couple of jerks were enough to send a creamy fountain of cum jetting high upwards. Pilar reached her own crisis simultaneously with piercing cries.

"*Maravilloso!*" she gasped. "Yes . . . yes!"

Tony just lay on the bed.

"I think," Pilar went on dreamily, her hand still playing softly with her clit. "We both could do with a rest now." They both lay still for a good ten minutes. Tony recovered gradually. As he revived, lying comfortably with his arms around Pilar, he felt a sudden yearning for something other than sex, he was hungry.

All that energy he'd expended was having its side effects, and he knew he could do with some food inside him. He wondered if Pilar might like to go out for a meal.

"Pilar," he whispered in her ear.

She stirred, and put her hand on his already stiffening cock.

"No, not yet" he said.

Pilar sat up, looking surprised.

"What then?" she said. "Don't you want to make some more love?"

"I'm hungry, would you like to go out for a meal?"

Pilar looked first astonished, then absolutely delighted. Clearly not so many of her customers invited her out, being mostly content with fucking her in the privacy of a hotel room.

"That would be marvellous, darling," she cried. "But I have no money Tony, I cannot pay anything for a meal."

"No problem," said Tony. "I'm paying. I'll put it down to expenses with my firm. You're a beautiful girl and you deserve a treat."

Pilar was just then lying very close to him as he spoke, and she put her face to his.

"Do I deserve a treat, Tony? Do I *querido*?" she purred, kissing him on the lips. "Then play with my pussy, please . . ."

She took his hand and placed his fingers on her clitoris. Tony started to rub, and just as he did so, a spurt of creamy white liquid squirted from her pussy. Pilar gave a little sigh of pleasure.

"That was nice, thank you," she whispered. "Now please excuse a moment. If we are going out, perhaps I put on my panties. This skirt is a little short for going out in."

"Just a little," Tony agreed with a grin.

She felt in a pocket in her skirt and pulled out her panties. Quickly she put them on as she lay on the bed.

"Now I am ready," she smiled, "where shall we go?"

"You decide," said Tony.

She took him to a secluded restaurant not far away, with private tables, low lighting and excellent food. As he gorged himself on Spanish lamb cutlets and a delicious assortment of vegetables from green peppers to avocado, he realised how hungry he was. Pilar smiled at him across the table as he ate, she had chosen a paella for herself with seafood and chicken. To drink, she had asked for a bottle of the house red, refreshing and quite strong.

As Tony ate he felt his sexual appetite returning. Pilar's smile was singularly erotic.

"Is your cock hard Tony?"

Tony nodded.

"Then I will suck you off."

Pilar slid down under the table. Tony could feel her fingers unbuttoning his trousers then pulling his zip down. Tugging his pants to one side she released his cock. Tony felt her moist lips cover the head, her tongue flicking back and forth across the tip. He looked around at the other people in the restaurant, most were eating and chatting, but then he noticed a woman sitting alone and she was looking straight at him. At first he dropped his gaze but after a few seconds looked up again. She was still staring at him. Then to his surprise the woman opened her mouth and slowly ran her tongue over her lips. Tony realised she must have seen Pilar slide under the table. Pilar was by now sucking him hard and fast, taking his cock to the back of her throat. Massaging his balls in her hands. Now the woman was sucking on a bread stick, her lips wrapped around it. This was all too much for Tony, his hot cum erupted into Pilar's mouth, his ejaculation seeming to last forever. Finally Pilar got back in her seat, wiping her mouth with a napkin.

"Have you been to Madrid before?" Pilar asked when she had to some extent recovered from her excitement.

"No, it's my first time."

"And with a girl to, I think . . ."

"No! Tony lied, seemingly indignant, "I've had lots of girls."

"But none as nice as me, no?"

"You're terrific," enthused the lad. "I'm here till the weekend. I'm a wine rep."

"Ah I see," said Pilar, holding his hand.

"Your English is very good, a lot better than my Spanish."

"I study English. This way I get 'a little bit on the side' you say?"

"Something like that," grinned Tony.

"Come on, I will show you La Puerta del Sol." Pilar said smiling.

It was quite dark by now, but everywhere the lights, the illuminated fountains and the rush of young people enjoying themselves made it sparkling and invigorating. Tony felt very happy and it was marvellous to feel the hand of this young girl in his as she led him across the square.

"You like porn?" she asked winking slyly. "There is some good porn here, but buy Spanish porn, it's cheaper than German or French and much better."

They were looking in the *Estancos* at the myriad of erotic magazines, some very expensive indeed and way beyond Tony's limited pocket.

"Here is a good one," said Pilar, pointing. "It is not too expensive and it is very sexy," she giggled. "Full of naked girls, and they do just about everything a girl can do. And that includes being fucked in the bum." She gave a silvery laugh that caused Tony's cock to stir again. "Tell me Tony," she whispered in his ear, not losing the chance to give it a lick. "Do you fancy seeing a very dirty movie? It would give us both great pleasure and with my help you will find it even more pleasurable."

Tony was willing to try anything once, and nodded; Pilar led the way to the nearest *Sala X*.

It was a bit of a sleazy dive, cheap and rather nasty, with about half a dozen dark shapes around the small room presumably bringing themselves off in response to what was happening on the screen. A little man with a large torch led Tony and Pilar to a convenient seat, and they struggled across a semi-recumbent form to find themselves places to some extent out of the way.

At last Tony was able to pay attention to what was going on; he was quite shocked. A young girl was sitting knickerless in a wood, masturbating. Her legs wide apart, she repeatedly plunged her fist into her cunt, while her free hand played with her tits, tweaking the nipples between her fingers. A lad of about sixteen was watching, cock in hand.

Tony had never seen anything as explicit as this in his life. His cock was throbbing like a dynamo, and the more he watched, the more he wanted to pull it out and afford himself some on the spot relief. It was here Pilar took him in hand. Slowly easing down his zip she felt for his aching dick.

"Lavely," she whispered. "What a beautiful cock you have Tony!"

Slowly she wanked him, rubbing his head of his cock with her thumb until he squirmed, while on the screen almost unnoticed, two lesbians were sucking each other out.

"You nearly ready to come Tony?" Pilar whispered in his ear.

"Very soon . . . oh now," replied Tony.

Pilar quickly took a tissue from her pocket and covered his cock. Tony came again, his cum spurting into the tissue. Pilar rolled the tissue up and threw it onto the floor.

Soon after, they got up and returned to the hotel. In anticipation of a sexy evening, Tony had purchased a bottle of whisky, and the two drank generous measures as they read through Tony's sex comic. His eyes and his cock shot up simultaneously, the latter somewhat impeded by the restriction of his trousers.

"Undress," Pilar encouraged, "you can enjoy porn better naked."

She was starting to take off her clothes, and it was a truly delectable sight to see her breasts become exposed, topped with raspberry pink nipples that she fondled and teased. Soon they were quite nude, and Pilar's hand found Tony's throbbing cock, while his played with her clit. They proceeded to enjoy each other and the magazine.

"Do you like my vertical smile?" she teased, lying back on the bed and opening her pussy with two fingers. Tony's cock stood horizontally before him. Pilar gently played with it while he played with her dark nipples.

"Now let me lick it," she breathed taking his cock in her hand. First she licked the tip, dropping saliva on to it and sucking it off, squeezing it tenderly between her lips. Then softly, she stroked and massaged it up and down with feather fingers, using her nails gently to scratch the tight skin. Tony's cock under her delicate ministrations stood flat against his stomach, enabling her easily to lick it underneath. He once more started heaving and tossing, arching his back off the bed.

"Shall I toss you off now?" she asked.

Unable to speak he dumbly nodded his cock felt white hot.

"Okay then, here goes," she said grasping his burning prick and jerking it up and down hard over and over again until it tossed off a volcanic eruption of thick cum.

Tony and Pilar lay together for a while, then Pilar spoke softly.

"Tony."

"Yes."

"Will you give me an English lesson?"

Tony looked at her, puzzled. "An English lesson? But why? Your English is very good . . ."

"Yes," said the girl, "but I want to know more. I want to know . . ." She paused and glanced mischievously at Tony.

"What?" he said.

"I want to know *parts of the body*!"

"I'd have thought you knew them already!"

"Yes, but not all of them, and I want to practice speaking them. Like, what is the English for this?" she asked pointing.

"Prick," Tony replied with a broad smile. "That's my prick."

"Preek?"

"No, *prick*, or cock."

"Cock," Pilar repeated. "I like cock."

"You can say that again. Do you want some cock now?"

His cock was beginning to rise to the occasion.

"No, no," exclaimed Pilar, "I want to learn more English first. Tell me what this is." She pointed.

"That's your cunt."

"Cant?"

"No, no it's cunt . . . cunt."

"Ah, *cont*!," she exclaimed in triumph.

"Not bad," Tony said with a laugh.

"Don't laugh," chided Pilar, "I do my best. What are these then?"

"Your tits."

"Teets?"

"Or breasts."

"I like English," she said nuzzling up close to Tony. "And you have a lavely preek." She began to play with it in her hand.

"Your *cant* isn't bad either," he said, stroking her a little so she parted her thighs.

"Play with me some more Tony," she sighed, turning

over. He pushed his thumb between her cheeks and felt her anus, feathering it until she squirmed.

"Mmm that's so nice," Tony she purred.

She turned on to her back, still playing with his cock and pulling the foreskin up and down. She lay back on the bed with her legs over her head, and she spread her pussy wide with her fingers, giving Tony an unrestricted view of her tight pussy. At once he slipped his penis into her like a knife into melted butter. He took hold of both her arms and held them tightly above her head. He thrust in and out pushing her into the mattress.

When Tony woke up Pilar's card lay on the bedside table. Pilar was gone and so was Tony's virginity.

Bettina writes,

I spend hours on the internet, there are so many sexy sites to visit. And there's always plenty of hot girly action. The following story is about a sizzling net babe, I'd sure like to link up with her . . .

Emma's World

EMMA'S WORLD

Emma reached behind her and unclipped something that allowed her skirt to fall to the floor. Her pussy was covered by a thin triangle of white satin tied up at the sides, just covering what I was dying for. I ran a hand through my hair and took a deep breath.

She stood about two metres from me and she looked like a goddess and a that moment I felt extremely unworthy. She was without doubt the most sizzling beautiful vision I have ever had the privilege to encounter. The website did not do her justice, in real life the blonde hair was gold and shiny. Her tight red top held her figure amazingly as her breasts tried to escape from their soft fabric prison.

She placed a hand on her hip and slid it round to the thin string that kept her hidden. She pulled it and it fell partially away, I could see a little of her as her knickers hung down. She slipped her hand between her legs and a finger disappeared inside her. She gasped and I strained. I gripped the arm of the sofa in frustration. My back arched and I contracted my arse muscles in an attempt to gain some control over my body.

"She's ready for you . . ." she said with a mild frown on her face that showed a mounting tension. The thought of fucking her made me feel ill with anticipation. And this was only the beginning of my day with Emma. I watched as she fondled herself gently. My trousers trapped my aching cock and I was dying to release it. She took a few steps towards me and I leaned forward. I pulled at the string on the other side of her panties and they fell to the floor leaving her completely exposed. I held her hips as she still used her hand to gently touch herself. I looked up at her, she was panting now, losing a little of the self control that up to now she had executed so expertly. I held her eyes in mine and wondered if I should just do what I wanted to do. Her email had said that it was my day, to do just as I wanted. . . so I leaned towards her and inserted the tip of my tongue between her legs and lightly flicked her clitoris. She squirmed in my hands, I was burning, exploding. The thought of putting myself inside her, filling her, fucking her, was like dynamite.

She pulled at her top, lifted it up over her head and exposed her breasts. I squeezed them and licked them over and over. I pulled her face to mine and my tongue entered her mouth exploring the first of the internal parts of her I was planning to explore. Her hands were opening my jeans and soon I was free of them. Her hand gently traced the mounting bulge in my shorts and I nearly came right then. My shorts fell to the floor. She pushed me back into the sofa and knelt between my legs. She rubbed her breasts on my cock and slid it between them. The feeling was overwhelming and I begged myself not to come . . not now I told myself . . not yet! Oh God - she was lowering herself - her mouth was an inch from my penis. I looked around the room for something to take my mind off coming. All I could see were the photographs of Emma all around the walls, of her mostly nearly naked and semi-orgasmic. Think of something, think of something!

The tip of my cock was against her lips. She paused and looked up at me.

"Suck me." I said. "Please."

I exhaled hard as her lips parted and engulfed me. She licked and sucked at me and I wanted it to go on forever. I dared to take a look as her head bobbed continuously in my lap. I played with her nipples and her eyes met mine, my breathing was out of control. She lifted her head from between my legs and climbed on to my lap. She knelt above me and I kissed her stomach and rubbed between her legs. Carefully, I pushed a finger inside her and she buckled as I entered. I held her just above my huge erection, the tip seemed to grow in an attempt to reach up into her. Emma's eyes were closed and a look of delight moved over her as I slowly pulled her down on my cock. I eased into her tight hole and held her hips tightly. I lifted her, pulled her down, over and over, I slipped in and out with such ease

"You're fucking me. Oh, that is . . . oh!" She was finding speech difficult. My heart was racing, my cock ready to burst. She writhed around, she was coming, coming sitting on me. I could feel my end coming as never before.

"Stop," she said, "I want the pleasure to last," and she

lifted herself off me.

"What?"

She got to her feet, turned away from me and bent over the arm of the couch, so that her bare arse begged to be fucked. Then I remembered her website said 'no anal'.

"Fuck me from behind."

I stared at her rear, her pussy was glistening with her juices. I stood behind her and smeared her buttocks with her wetness. I didn't hold back this time. I thrust myself into her. I throbbed inside her, I threw myself into her pussy over and over, harder and harder, I grunted and groaned as I watched my cock fuck her. She came quickly, she knew what she wanted and she got it, hard. I slapped against her, my balls squashed against her arse. I pushed her legs wide apart and satisfied myself to the full. I lifted her from the floor with every thrust. As I came I saw heaven, my mind blew as I spurted all I could into her open pussy. I gripped her hips with all my might and I felt for a second as though I didn't exist anymore. Streaming into her, filling her.

I was finished. I pulled out of her and fell to the floor in exhaustion. "Phew!" I said. She stepped over me and I saw her sopping pussy, my cum oozing, dripping down the inside of her thighs.

She covered herself with a towel from the radiator. I lie naked and spent on the lounge rug.

The doorbell rang. I jumped to my feet. "Who the hell's that?"

That'll be Rebecca, a friend of mine. She'll want to

fuck you too. And I haven't finished with you yet. Would you like to fuck us both?"

Before I could answer she left the room. I sat on the sofa and covered myself with a cushion. The door opened.

"This is Rebecca."

She took off her clothes and walked slowly towards me. Thank God for the internet.

She pulled the cushion away fell to her knees and buried her head between my legs.

Bettina writes,

Now that playtime is nearly over it's time to go back to school. These girls have an assignment to complete if they are going to get their O levels, and they're keen to get an A grade.

Pay attention now, you won't want to miss anything . . .

Stage School

STAGE SCHOOL

I clicked on 'Get Mail' and there it was. My invitation. It read:

Hi Jim,

Thanks for your email, it was lovely to hear from you, Melanie and I are really looking forward to meeting you, and I promise you will be more than well looked after here with us. You'll have one of the best experiences of your life. We promise!!!

The evening consists of a 'live' and very explicit hardcore girl/girl sex show starring Melanie and myself Tina, and is strictly for adults only. Our show includes deep french kissing, toys galore, oral sex and full-on sex with a strap-on, mutual masturbation to full orgasms (we do cum for real, no faking) plus lots more.

The evening lasts for about three hours. The main floor show lasting over an hour. This will be followed by us interacting with you our guests, posing for photos and having a real sexy time. The guest list is limited to six so you will have our total attention.

The theme for the evening is 'schoolgirls' so we will be dressed accordingly. The show will be held in a secluded country house, obviously I can't give you the address until we have received payment. The total cost for an evening of sex beyond your wildest dreams is £300.

Attached to this email is a photo of me, I'm sure you will agree that I am well worth the money. We promise you an evening you will never forget. I look forward to meeting you in person on the night. Please email me back if you are interested and I will tell you about the payment methods and then the venue.   Hope to see you very soon.

Lots of love and kisses Tina xxx

I returned the email straight away and was sent back instructions on how to pay. And when I'd paid I was given details of where and when. It was all very secretive and underhand, but that only added to my excitement.

The day finally arrived. I couldn't get the idea of meeting and maybe fucking Melanie or Tina or even fucking both of them out of my mind. Tina had emailed me her photo and everyone in England knew Melanie. She was one of the country's top glamour models who had been in every tabloid newspaper, and was a regular on late night adult satellite TV. This evening was going to be amazing!

I arrived early and sat in my car outside a fairly large Victorian detached house, number eighteen Prospect Place, I'd found it.

Opening the glove compartment I pulled out a few girly mags. I always keep a couple handy in case I get stuck in a traffic jam. As luck would have it staring up at me seductively was Melanie. On the cover she was dripping wet. Water gushed over her breasts from what looked like a fireman's hose, which she was holding with both hands. The strap line was 'Push your pole into my soaking snatch'. I thumbed my way past 'Readers Wives', a beautiful spread of 'Crystal's Tips' and a lovely layout of a sexy nineteen year old called 'Sandy' pictured laying on virginal white sheets, her legs wide and two fingers spreading her pussy wide open. She had the most innocent look on her face. As if she was totally unaware of the effect she would be having on the readers. She certainly had an effect on me.

I turned a few more pages and found Melanie on page sixty-four. Thick shoulder length auburn hair, big blue eyes and lips that were made to suck dicks, my dick I thought, hopefully in a few hours time. And those breasts. The caption read 36CC, but they looked bigger to me, they had to be at least a double D, surely. She was the perfect, fuckable, made to measure woman.

She was pictured in a fire-station, naked except for a fireman's helmet leaning back against a fire truck, legs parted fucking herself with two fingers.

I could hardly believe that in less than half an hour it would be real and not a photo.

I then remembered that on page sixty-nine of this particular magazine they always have a photo of a girl sucking some lucky guy's cock. I quickly turned the pages and there was Melanie squatting in front of this guy, one hand squeezing his arse the other caressing his balls, her lips wrapped around his thick shaft. In the shot on the opposite page her tongue licked at the very tip, you could see her saliva glistening around its head. I turned over and her tits were covered in cum, and she was looking straight out of the pages at me. I knew my three hundred pounds had been well spent.

I closed the magazine and slipped it back in the glove compartment. I looked at my watch, it was seven forty-five.

I walked up the pathway and rang the bell. The door

was opened by a young girl. It wasn't Melanie or Tina. She was wearing a white blouse with a neck-tie and a very short gymslip style dress. Her hair was in pigtails and she had freckles painted on her face.

"Hello I'm Jim," I said nervously.

"Well hello Jim, my name's Nadia." Nadia stepped forward and kissed me on the cheek. "Let me take your jacket, are you here for the show?"

"Yes, I'm a few minutes early, but it's better than being late."

She took my coat. Then she pushed herself right up against me and whispered. "Follow me Jim, I'll show you my secret room."

We'd only walked a few steps when she stopped and opened the door to the cupboard under the stairs. She reached in and switched on the light, then disappeared inside.

"Are you coming in?" she said from inside the cupboard.

I peered inside. I was surprised to see her bending over a small school desk, the type used in junior schools. Her naked arse in the air and her legs parted revealing her pussy.

"What are you waiting for, you can do what ever you like with me . . . cane me, smack me, eat me, fuck me. There's a cane in the corner and some condoms in that dish."

I closed the door behind me. I couldn't believe this was happening to me. I thought I would wake up any minute. She could see I was hesitating.

"What would you like me to do?" I said, trying to be polite.

"I think I need a good smack. I've been a very naughty girl today."

I picked up the cane.

"Please smack me with your bare hand, it feels so much nicer."

I put down the cane, and positioned myself behind her. I rested one hand in the small of her back and lightly smacked her with the other.

"I've been a very, very bad girl, I deserve a good *hard* smacking."

I brought my hand back and slapped her cheeks with a little more force this time.

"Ouch!"

"I'm sorry . . . I didn't mean to hurt you," I stammered, apologizing.

"No, that was lovely, smack me again. This time a bit harder."

Nadia arched her back so her arse stuck out even more. Again I hit her. And again.

"Arrgh . . . ouch! Ooh yes that was nice. Feel my pussy it's so hot and wet."

I put my hand down between her legs, she was red hot and wet.

"Now, I need to be fucked . . . here put one of these condoms on and fuck me."

In all of my thirty-seven years a girl had never said

those words to me. I undid my zip and pulled out my erect cock. Nadia tore open the packet with her teeth, she handed me the condom.

"You have a beautiful cock Jim," she said looking down.

I held the end of the rubber and slowly rolled it up my penis. I don't think it had ever been so big.

"That's it," she said. "Now fuck me . . . I want you to fuck me right now."

Nadia bent over the desk again and opened her legs as far as she could. The sight of her arse and open pussy really made me want to fuck her so badly. I took hold of my cock and guided it into her juicy tight cunt. Grabbing both her butt cheeks I pushed myself into her.

"Yes, that's it," she sighed. "I need it . . . fuck me good."

I watched my cock slide in and out. She had the sexiest arse and beautiful smooth soft skin. Only the rubber stopped me from coming too soon. If I hadn't been wearing it I'm sure I would have shot my load immediately, Nadia was so fucking sexy.

"Deeper," she said.

I pressed down on her arse to go in deeper.

"Oh that's it," she said. "Fuck me harder."

I thrust harder into her.

"Come on baby, you can do it harder than that. I want you to hurt me."

I slapped against her, banging her harder and faster holding nothing back. The desk was rocking. We were fucking wildly.

"Yeah baby . . . ooh, that feels good. Your dick feels so big . . . ooh it's so big . . ."

As Nadia came she cried out and I fucked her as fast and as hard as I could, her body lifting off the desk with every thrust and her butt cheeks wobbling as I slapped against them, hammering into her. Her screaming made me come too, her tight cunt sucking the cream out of me.

I pulled out of her and Nadia turned round. She looked down at my still erect cock, and taking it in her hand she slipped off the condom.

"Ooh it looks like you haven't had sex for a long while!" she said dropping it in the bin. "That was lovely wasn't it. I hope you enjoy the rest of the evening."

Nadia straightened her dishevelled pigtails and pulled down her gym slip to cover up that beautiful arse. She opened the door and peered round it to see if anyone was about.

"All clear," she said, as if we really weren't supposed to be in there. I felt guilty as if I'd done something I shouldn't, something really naughty, like I used to feel when I was at school.

I followed her to a room across the hall.

"Now, make yourself comfortable in here. Sit on one of the sofas that are free and the girls will be with you shortly."

The room was quite spacious, and the decor plush. The colours of the room were subdued and rich, and the lighting slightly low. There were six sofas arranged around a small stage which was positioned in the middle of the room. On the stage was a blue deep pile carpet. The sofas were large and comfortable and covered in a soft crushed velvet and scattered with large cushions. Four guys were in the room already sitting on a sofa each. There were lamps on small tables and a dark wooden floor. I sat down. The doorbell rang.

"Ooh the last guest," said Nadia smiling, "excuse me while I answer that." She quickly left the room. The other four guys weren't speaking, just drinking. They each had their own table with a drink. I poured myself a drink too and sat back.

A few minutes later I could hear Nadia screaming with pleasure again, and then after a short while she appeared in the doorway with the sixth guy who came in and sat down with us. Looking at him and the others, I realised that I was probably the most good looking man in the room which I thought couldn't do me any harm. Nadia got up on the small stage.

"I hope you all enjoyed me guys. I enjoyed every one of you. I hope you come again soon - I know you will when Mel and Tina do their thing. Well I'll love you and leave you all for now . . . bye." Nadia did a childish theatrical curtsey and skipped out of the room.

We each sat on our sofas and nobody said a word. We sat in silence for about ten minutes and I was beginning to feel slightly uncomfortable. I looked round at the guy nearest to me. He stared straight ahead drinking from his glass every now and then. It was like each of us was cocooned in our own space, in our own world and not in the same room at all.

Then someone must have switched on a sound system as some music began playing. Melanie and Tina appeared in the doorway dressed in their schoolgirl outfits. Their clothes were small and tight-fitting, hugging their womanly curves and they looked stunningly sexy. Their blouses were white and stretched tightly over their full breasts, their nipples clearly visible through the thin material. Melanie's blouse was tied at the waist showing a midriff of tanned skin. Tina's blouse was tucked tightly into her waistband. Their tiny skirts were dark green and pleated. They both wore school ties untidily knotted round their collars. Both girls were beautiful and their makeup perfect, their lips painted a bright glossy red. Tina's long blonde hair was styled in two plaits, and Melanie wore an alice band in her auburn hair. They both looked great, so girly and cute.

As they paused in the doorway, Tina slowly lowered herself to a crouching position and ran her hands up the outside of Melanie's legs lifting her skirt slightly. She worked her hands further over Melanie's body and breasts and kissed her gently and softly on the lips, lingering there for a moment.

Coming into the room they danced in a slow rhythm from sofa to sofa. Melanie took my glass and sipped my drink, smiling sexily at me, then replaced the glass on the table. Both girls moved around between the sofas, lifting their skirts and wiggling their arses at us on their way up on to the stage. They looked so hot I was getting an erection already.

"Hello boys! I'm Tina as I think most of you will know. I hope Nadia has looked after you well, she loves our little evening get-togethers. She's very enthusiastic isn't she? Melanie and I are pleased to see you all, and looking round I can see you are all so very handsome too. We're lucky tonight aren't we Melanie?"

"We sure are. Hi boys, I'm Melanie, I'm feeling so hot and horny tonight and I can't *wait* to do the show for you. I hope you are all sitting comfortably because we are about to begin . . ."

I took a sip of my drink. Then the music quietened and a female voice came over the sound system.

'Once upon a time there were two schoolgirls, Melanie and Tina. They were great friends and shared all their secrets. They were very naughty schoolgirls, and were always getting into trouble. They were often to be seen outside the headmistress's room waiting for a spanking, or having to stay after school in detention for their bad behaviour . . .'

Melanie and Tina posed on the stage as the words were spoken. At the word 'naughty' they lifted their skirts showing us their small white panties. And they bent over at the word 'spanking' putting their hands flat on the floor but keeping their legs straight.

'One day they were in Tina's bedroom looking at the poster of their best boy band and dreaming of what sex would be like with them . . .'

The room lights went down and two spotlights lit the stage. Melanie and Tina stood in the middle of the stage and pretended to look up at a poster.

"Hey Tina, I think I'd *definitely* give my cherry to *him*. If I was going to do it, I would let him be the first. He'd be the first one to touch me and I'd let him fuck me over and over."

"Melanie, you are *so* bad, don't let my parents hear you talk like that. Anyway I don't think I would let him do that to me, I'd prefer someone a bit more mature. Someone who knew what they were doing. Like maybe Mr White, I've always fancied him."

"What, our English teacher?"

"Yeah, he's dreamy," said Tina pushing a hand between her legs. "In his class I try to sit at the front, and then I open my legs to let him see my underwear. I'm sure he's noticed. And when I get home from school I can't wait to get to my room to play with myself, and I imagine what it would be like to be with him. I pretend that I'm lying back on his desk and he's on top of me, pushing his big cock into me . . ."

"I know what you mean," said Melanie, "every day when I get home, before my tea, I go to my room, but instead of doing my homework I do this . . ."

Melanie lifted up her short skirt and put her hand inside her panties. Her eyes met mine. She winked and smiled at me. I smiled back. Her fingers disappeared inside the thin white cotton fabric. "I love to stroke my hot pussy till I come."

"Let me look," said Tina.

Melanie fingered herself as Tina dropped to her knees to watch. Tina pulled down Melanie's panties and she stepped out of them. Tina threw them on the table in front of me. I picked them up, they were wet.

"Ooh your pussy is so beautiful Melanie."

"If you want you can kiss it," Melanie said opening her legs a little.

Tina leaned forward and put her mouth between Melanie's legs. Her tongue delved between the pussy lips and disappeared. My cock was so hard watching them, I just wanted them to come down to my sofa and work on my cock for a while. I wanted to fuck both of them, they were so sexy.

"Oh Tina that feels so good, your tongue inside my pussy, it's so warm and it's moving so fast, you'd better stop before I come."

Tina sat back on her heels and rubbed her hands over her smooth thighs. "You know what, sometimes I creep into my mum's room and take one of her vibrators out of the drawer. They are so much fun, we could use one now, shall I get one?"

"Yeah, get it now."

Tina left the stage, leaving Melanie still standing with her skirt raised, fingering her cunt. She looked around at us.

"You can get your dicks out if you like boys," Melanie said smiling, "we don't mind." None of us took her up on the offer, although I really wanted to, but I didn't want to be the first. "Don't be shy. There's some tissues on the tables if you need them during the evening," Melanie encouraged but without avail.

Tina reappeared and jumped back up on the stage.

"These are my mum's," she said opening a bag and tipping out a selection of sex toys. There was a silver vibrator, a big black dildo and a strap-on.

"Ooh let's try this one first." Melanie pointed to the vibrator. "It's the prettiest of all."

Both girls knelt down. Melanie held the vibrator and sitting back on her bottom turned it on and rubbed it up and down her thighs. I could just hear the faint buzzing over the music.

"I won't get an electric shock will I Tina?"

"No silly, I've used it hundreds of times."

Melanie took it closer to her pussy and opened her legs a little more. She pressed it against her clitoris, and threw back her head as she began to enjoy the feel of it vibrating against her. I wanted to fuck her, I wanted to spread her legs apart and push my aching cock inside that tight cunt, she'd got me the hardest I'd been for a long time. The stage began to rotate very slowly. Melanie slipped the tip of the vibrator inside her and gradually she moved from my sight. I couldn't wait for her to come round in front of me, I strained my neck to see her long silky legs apart on the floor. I wanted to be between them. Tina undid Melanie's blouse and opened it. Melanie's stunning breasts were upright and the nipples stuck right out. Tina licked them, then caressed them with her fingers. With her other hand, Tina pulled up the back of her skirt and pulled down her panties halfway down her thighs so I had a good view of her arse and pussy. I wanted to finger her. My hand slipped down to press on my cock, how much more could I take without release.

I noticed some movement out of the corner of my eye and the man opposite me on the other side of the stage suddenly got up. Cock in hand he strode on to the stage.

"Look at me cock girlzz . . . don't you want it then?" his words were slurred, he'd had one drink too many. He stood there tossing himself off. The girls looked a bit alarmed.

"Well c'mon then, I'm ready for ya, who wants it first?" He proudly brandished his cock at them.

Melanie stood up. "Hey, you're not part of the show you know, I think you'd better sit down - if not you'll have to leave."

The drunk guy had other ideas. He knelt down dramatically beside Tina, and like some porn star he exaggerated his hand movements, rubbing his cock, and screwing up his face to show everyone how good he was at wanking. I could see the girls needed some help with this one. I got up and went up on the stage. Tina had moved away and I grabbed the guy's arm to encourage him to exit.

"Come on then mate, show's over. It's time you were on your way isn't it?" Just then another man appeared at the doorway. I hadn't seen him before. One of the girls must have called him somehow. He came straight over, picked the guy up, dragged him to the front door and threw him out. Melanie came over to me and kissed me on the cheek, "Hey thanks for that, he had me worried there for a minute. We don't get much of that really, most of our guests are well-behaved, and usually act like gentlemen. Thanks for your help."

"That's okay," I said, "any time." It felt good to get special attention from Melanie. She walked back to my table with me, poured herself a drink and took a mouthful.

"Sorry for that rude interruption boys. Now let's get on with the show."

The girls were soon back on the stage. They sat down on the carpet and started to kiss deeply. The stage began to turn. Their hands caressed each other, moving from their breasts, down between their legs, every inch of their bodies. Melanie lay back, her legs wide. Tina was on top sucking Melanie's breasts, squeezing them with her hands and biting her nipples, flicking them with her tongue. Melanie was enjoying it and my erection was back, the incident forgotten.

"Fuck me with that," Melanie said pointing at the strap-on. "Be gentle with me, it's my first time." She smiled.

Tina sat up and took off her skirt and blouse. She slipped off her panties and was now naked except for her high heeled shoes. She picked up the dildo and tied the strap around her waist, fastening it tightly. Melanie positioned herself on all fours, her cunt wanton. Tina knelt behind her. She guided the rubber cock so it was only inches from Melanie's tight entrance.

I glanced over, through the darkness and saw that the guy next to me had his cock in his hand, masturbating slowly as he watched. I was desperate to do the same but still held on to too many inhibitions.

Tina inserted the tip of the strap-on into Melanie's pussy.

"Ooh that's amazing . . . it's so big. It's really stretching me. I'll open my legs wider so you can push it in deeper."

Melanie opened her legs and the stage turned so that my view of her pussy was straight on. It was beautiful and glistened in the spotlights. Tina was pushing the strap-on very slowly into Melanie, pulling out a bit and then pushing in again, each time it went in further.

"Come on, give it to me baby . . ." Melanie whispered, and Tina increased the force of her actions. Soon Tina's forward motion saw the strap-on disappearing right inside Melanie's cunt. I thought I was going to have to leave the room to masturbate, my cock was stretched to bursting and throbbing under my zip. I pressed down on it again trying to alleviate the frustration. I wanted to be behind Melanie in Tina's place, fucking her, touching her, and hear her tell *me* to give it to her. The stage revolved again and I saw Melanie's face as she was fucked by the strap-on. She was enjoying it, she was moving herself back on to it with each thrust. Tina grasped Melanie's hair and pulled it gently backwards as she thrust inside her. That seemed to excite Melanie even more and she arched her back in response.

"Faster baby faster, fuck me faster . . ."

Her words spoke directly to my cock and I couldn't help but slide it out of my fly to squeeze the shaft and friction it, and fuck Melanie faster and faster . . .

Tina increased the speed of her fucking and Melanie started to come. Her gasps and cries had me ejaculating into a tissue. There were sighs and groans coming from all around the room.

The girls didn't stop though. The strap-on was thrown to one side and Melanie picked up the big black dildo.

"It's your turn now Tina," she said and motioned to her to lie on her back on the carpet.

"Ooh that looks big, I'll never get that inside my tight cunt."

"Well then I'll have to make sure you are good and wet before I use it on you won't I. Now lie down there and open your legs wide."

Tina lay on her back and spread her legs wide like she'd been told. Melanie's hands moved over Tina's breasts and pinched the nipples before she sucked on them. Then the girls kissed deeply, and Melanie's tongue was inside Tina's mouth and probing. Melanie was definitely taking the lead this time, and she slid her hand down to tease Tina's pussy.

"Ooh I love your pussy Tina, I'll just lick you before I fuck you."

Melanie moved down and pressed the tip of her tongue

onto Tina's clitoris. She made sure we could see what she was doing, spreading the pussy lips with her fingertips, American style. Tina squirmed under her, and her wriggling was sending the blood back to my prick. Melanie began to really suck Tina's pussy and Tina squeezed and caressed her own nipples, licking her lips, she looked so fuckable.

"Hey, you're *so* wet now, I think it's time to fuck you."

"Yes, fuck me Melanie, please fuck me now."

Melanie reached out slowly for the black dildo. She put the tip of it inside her mouth and gave it the beginnings of a blow job to make it nice and wet.

"Ooh Melanie put it inside me now, come on, I'm ready . . . please."

Melanie held open Tina's pink pussy lips and pushed the black dildo in. It went in slowly but in one go.

"You're so wet Tina . . . it's gone right in."

Melanie fucked Tina and kissed her again all the while the dildo went in and out. It must have been a good ten inches. Tina turned over, her head resting on the fluffy carpet, her arms out in front of her and her arse was high in the air.

"Spread your legs wider Tina, wider."

Tina knees slid further apart and Melanie again pushed the dildo in. Tina let out a gasp.

"Oh it's so big, it's filled me, and it's so long . . . and ah, oh . . . so thick"

It was obvious Tina was talking about *my* dick, and I was definitely filling her right now as I took the base of my cock between my fingers and slid my other hand up its length. No, I thought, I'd better not come again, I'd better save some for Melanie later.

"How does that feel?" said Melanie as she made the strokes slower and longer. The dildo nearly came out as she pulled it backwards, then it went right inside again.

"Ooh it feels so nice, I love a long . . . slow . . . fuck . . . it's so tight inside my cunt, it's so . . . ooh!"

"Shall I make you come now?" Melanie asked.

"Yes please . . . make me come . . ."

Melanie's left hand pinched and played with Tina's clitoris while her right hand expertly fucked her with the dildo.

"Oh I'm going to come . . . yes . . . ooh . . . yes, yes!"

Tina's orgasm sent more blood to my cock, she wriggled and gasped and Melanie thrust the dildo into her, massaging and pulling on her clit. Tina thrashed around in ecstacy, out of control, her fingers tearing at the carpet.

"There that's better isn't it Tina, now you've had a good fuck."

Tina lay back rubbing, caressing her body and breasts tenderly with her fingertips as she came down from her orgasm.

"Ooh that was wonderful Melanie, you really know how to make me come."

The girls got up.

"Well boys," began Melanie, "that's the end of this part of the evening. Give me and Tina a minute and we'll be back to see you shortly."

The girls grabbed their clothes and sex toys and disappeared out of the door. My cock was left unsatisfied and aching to fuck. I couldn't wait to see the girls come back and it wasn't long before they reappeared.

They were back in all their schoolgirl gear and they came across to the sofas. Tina went over to a nearby guy and Melanie sat down next to me.

"Hi Jim."

"Hello Melanie." I felt a bit shy, I wasn't expecting her to sit right next to me when she came out.

"Are you having a good time?"

"Yes, I loved the floor show."

"We may do a bit more in a minute, it depends if we find a guy willing to go up and join in for the last set. It looks like Tina is finding out if they are interested."

Tina went to another sofa, obviously finding no luck with the first. I was hoping Melanie wouldn't ask me to go up, I didn't feel like having an audience myself.

"Did we turn you on Jim?"

"You sure did."

"Did you want to fuck us?"

"Yes."

"That's good, we hope to turn all our guests on."

Tina took the hand of a guy and pulled him up from the sofa. She guided him up to the stage, he looked a bit unwilling. Tina looked across at Melanie and there was some sort of message understood between them.

"Tina's going to handle this one herself," Melanie told

me. "I want to stay with you." She got close to me and made herself comfortable on the sofa.

"Pour me a drink Jim, and let's enjoy Tina's show."

I did as she asked, and sat back feeling pleased with myself. I must have made some impression on her during the evening.

On the stage Tina danced around the guy while some music played, and she ran her fingers down his fly to trace the bulge of his erection. Out of her pocket she pulled a small condom packet, and made it a part of her performance to open it with her teeth, place the condom in her mouth, and then turn her attention to the guy's erection. She slowly unzipped his fly and put her hand inside to free his penis. She held it in her hands and put her mouth to it's tip. I felt for the guy, what if he shoots his load right now, he must be on the edge. Her mouth slowly covered his prick with the condom, and when it emerged from her lips it was perfectly covered with the rubber. Then she started to give him a slow and deep blow job. I don't know how he kept going, she was so beautiful, and the sight of her moving too and fro in front of his fly, and her red lips wrapped around the girth of his cock would be too much for most men to bear. My own erection was in full force again and I felt Melanie's hand begin to rub my thigh.

"Do you like to watch Tina giving head?"

"Yeah, she's great."

"Look at that cock sliding in and out of her mouth. She's so good at it. Her tongue is busy too, round the head and down the shaft. She'll give that guy a *real* good time. Would you like to see me giving head too?"

I looked at Melanie. I was getting hot. Was she toying or did she really mean it.

"I'm serious, I love to give blow jobs. I love to feel a huge cock in my mouth, take it right to the back of my throat, feel it sliding down my tongue, coming in my mouth, then I swallow every bit . . ."

I knew she was teasing now because Tina was using a condom. These girls wouldn't do it without, would they? I wanted Melanie to take me in her mouth and suck me dry.

"Well what do you think Jim? Have you got anything for me?" Her hand slid to my prick and rubbed it. It pressed upwards towards her hand, trying to get to her mouth.

Slowly Melanie unzipped my fly. The guy on the stage was groaning and it seemed unlikely he could hold out much longer. Melanie took my hard cock in her soft hands. She massaged it up and down its length.

"Ooh it's so big and hard, you must want it bad. Do you want me to suck it for you?" I wanted her to stop teasing and do it now. She rubbed some more.

"What a beautiful cock. I'd love to suck it and have it shoot its cum into my mouth." If she didn't do something soon it was going to come in her hand right now.

Then I saw Melanie's head lower into my lap and I felt her warm lips touch the end of it. Licking, teasing, kissing. Gradually she allowed a little more of it inside her mouth. I pushed upwards wanting it all inside, wanting her take it all inside her mouth. Then she suddenly released my cock.

"Now I've seen that you've got self control, would you like to fuck me on stage? Then after that, I'll suck you until you're hard again, and you can come in my mouth. Would you like that Jim?"

The guy on stage had his cock free of the condom. He was naked from the waist down which looked strange with his neat shirt and tie. Tina was laying on her back and he was fucking her tits. It was only a few seconds before he ejaculated, his cum spurting, covering her face and breasts. She massaged his cream around her breasts and licked her lips.

Tina got up and took some tissues from a table. Wiping herself down she offered some to the guy in case he needed them.

"Now it's my turn," said Melanie, pulling me up on to the stage. We stood facing each other. She took my hands and placed them on her arse. She kissed me full on the lips, pushing her tongue into my mouth, and turning her head to the side in an exaggerated fashion so her hair hung down and she looked really good for the audience.

"Lift up my skirt," she whispered to me. I felt the soft material of her short skirt and pulled it up.

"Feel my arse Jim, isn't it lovely to touch?"

I felt the warm cotton stretched tightly over her bottom.

"Pull my knickers down."

I eased down her panties, and her skin was silky under my fingers as I caressed her backside and cupped her buttocks gently.

Melanie began to unzip my trousers, and then she helped me out of them. I forgot about what lay beyond the stage, all I could see was Melanie. She slowly undid her blouse, slipping it off so she was again naked in her high heels. Her legs were long and smooth and I wanted them wrapped around my waist, my cock spearing her, fucking her. Melanie turned around so her bare backside rubbed up against my prick still trapped in my boxers. She leant forward and touched her toes, her legs perfectly straight. Standing up, she took my hands and pulled my arms round her body, guiding my fingers down between her legs. Opening her thighs a little she pressed my fingers to her.

"Touch me Jim . . . finger my pussy. Make me nice and wet for your cock to slide in." Her teasing words had my cock throbbing and more than restless. I touched her clit and she squirmed in my arms, her curvy bottom wriggling tantalizingly against my hard erection. I slid my fingers further to the entrance of her cunt. She was soaked.

Melanie encouraged me to lie down on my back. My stiff prick at forty-five degrees.

"I'm going to get fucked now boys, are you all watching me? I'm going to have this beautiful cock inside me, pumping into me, giving it to me, fucking me hard and good . . ."

As Melanie spoke for the benefit of the other guys I wanted her to get down onto my prick fast, before I shot my load into the air. Her words were just exciting me too much and I squeezed the base of my cock trying to delay till I got inside her.

Finally Melanie rolled a condom over my erection. 'Just hold out a bit longer,' I said to myself. She sat astride me, gradually letting my cock squeeze between her pussy lips. Her cunt was so tight I forgot about the condom, it felt so good to get inside her, so hot. She rode me and I fondled her breasts. They felt wonderfully firm in my hands. She was enjoying fucking me - enjoying being in control. She licked her lips and her mouth was open, her head back. I just knew she was loving the feel of my stiff prick penetrating her tight cunt - she wasn't faking her pleasure for the other guys to watch. She took my hand and pushed three fingers in her mouth, she sucked them as she rode me, harder now and faster, and I knew I couldn't help but come this time. As I came, she must have felt my spasms inside her, she put my hand on her clit and I rubbed, bringing her off in seconds, making her wriggle and buck. She collapsed, exhausted, falling on top of me.

Afterwards Melanie slipped the condom off my prick. I wondered how I would manage another erection after that.

"Tina, come and help me for this one," said Melanie beckoning to Tina who was on a guy's lap. Tina came to the stage and Melanie whispered to her. Both girls got down on the floor and both took up positions on all fours.

"Tina, lick me out please," said Melanie opening her thighs to show her pussy and arse from behind. Tina began to lick Melanie's pussy, rubbing her hands over Melanie's arse and thighs as she probed her tongue around Melanie's clitoris. Mclanie looked up at me, sighing with the pleasure Tina was giving her.

"Jim come here, I want to suck your cock while Tina eats me."

Melanie pulled down my boxers and took my semierect penis in her hand.

"Ooh baby, c'mon get nice and stiff for me . . ." Melanie rubbed my cock and began to lick the shaft as it became erect in her hands.

"Ooh that's better, nice and hard. I want it in my mouth, I want to feel your cum spurt into my throat . . ."

Melanie's lips covered the end of my penis. It became harder inside her mouth.

"Ooh baby . . . that's better . . . it's getting bigger . . ."

As she spoke she squeezed my shaft in her hand, preparing to take my cock in her mouth again.

"It's so beautiful, it's so big and stiff . . ."

Melanie's lips once again let my cock between them and she looked up at me.

"Ooh Tina suck me, eat me, lick my pussy . . ."

My cock once again slipped between those lips. Letting me thrust deep into her mouth this time and get into a rhythm for a number of strokes.

"Ooh Tina suck me . . . lick me out . . ." cried Melanie.

Tina carried on with her attention to Melanie's pussy while Melanie allowed me back inside her mouth. This time she really sucked on my prick. Her sucking was rhythmic and so sexy, her head bobbing up and down, her lips sliding the length of my shaft. Her mouth was warm and tight around my cock, her tongue undulating. I couldn't hold back. I came in her mouth spurting my cream right to the back of her throat. My knees buckled. She sucked on me right till the last drop, swallowing it all.

"Mmm," she said, licking her lips. "There was still so much, even after you came at least twice before this evening."

I pulled up my boxers and put on my trousers. Tina and Melanie sat together on the carpet.

"Well, boys that's the entertainment for tonight," said Melanie.

"We hope you have had a good time and will come back again soon," Tina said smiling. "We'll just slip into our full outfits one last time, in case any of you boys want a photo taken with us before you leave. We can do some topless shots with you too if you like. Tina straightened her skirt and bent to collect her knickers from the stage.

I watched Melanie dress. She was a stunningly beautiful girl. I fantasized that I'd had a special effect on her, that she'd want me to come back and just fuck her alone one night, no guys, no show, just her and I.

Melanie came over to me.

"You were great - you've got a lot of stamina."

"Thanks, you were pretty good up there yourself," I said trying to be extra cool.

"I'd love to see you again," she said smiling sexily.

I'd cracked it. I gave her my usual charming smile. I

was obviously the cool guy I thought I was all along.

"Perhaps you'll come to our next gig in Bristol, see Tina I'm sure there's some tickets left."

Dear Reader,

Now that you have read my third collection I hope that you are fully satisfied. And I hope you didn't climax too soon!

Till next time . . .
Lots of love,

credits . . .

All other stories related by
Bettina Varese.

Coming soon . . . .

A special hardback
of adult Bedtime Stories
from Bettina

MAILING LIST
PLEASE SEND ME INFORMATION
ABOUT NEW PUBLICATIONS
LIMITED EDITIONS
SPECIAL OFFERS

NAME ....

ADDRESS ....

....

....

....

POSTCODE...

COUNTRY ....

e-mail:

Please return this slip to:

Bettina Varese
c/o COLLECTIVE PUBLISHING
P. O. BOX 6685
NEWARK
NG24 4WS
ENGLAND U.K.

Please see reverse for book ordering details

COLLECTIVE
PUBLISHING

sugar-coated babies
on a trashed-out trip to nowhere

destination
pulp